ALSO BY LILIANA RHODES

His Every Whim
His Every Whim, Part 1
His One Desire, Part 2
His Simple Wish, Part 3
His True Fortune, Part 4
The Billionaire's Whim - Boxed Set

Canyon Cove Billionaires
Playing Games
No Regrets
Second Chance
Hearts Collide
Perfect Together

Made Man Trilogy
Soldier
Capo
Boss
Dante - Boxed Set

The Crane Curse Trilogy
Charming the Alpha
Resisting the Alpha
Needing the Alpha
The Crane Curse Trilogy Boxed Set

Wolf at Her Door

His Immortal Kiss

Published by
Jaded Speck Publishing
5042 Wilshire Blvd #30861
Los Angeles, CA 90036

His Immortal Kiss
ISBN 978-1-939918-24-6

HIS IMMORTAL KISS

NEW YORK TIMES AND USA TODAY BESTSELLING AUTHOR
LILIANA RHODES

DEDICATION

To my son,
whatever you dream, you can do
I love you.

CHAPTER 1

I wiped the tears from my cheeks as I sank into the large soft seat of my Pontiac Bonneville. It was a sunny June day in central Virginia. I shouldn't have been sitting in my car crying. Unfortunately, I found myself there more and more often.

I opened a browser on my phone and flipped through my bookmarks looking for the one thing that always cheered me up - photographs of Chateau du Soleil. I had been obsessed with the building since I was a child. Sometimes Mom used to drive past it on the way home from school when I was younger. No matter what we did in school, driving past that castle was always the highlight of my day.

Chateau du Soleil was a 19th century Victorian castle that had been brought over from France, piece by piece, two hundred years ago. I had never been in the building before, but something about the way the sun reflected off the slim stained glass windows made it feel like home to me.

I flipped through the pictures online, expanding some so I could see the detail better while passing others I had seen time and time again. I was always on the lookout for new pictures of it, especially of the interior, but those were extremely rare.

My phone started to vibrate and sing as the timer went off.

Damn, has it been fifteen minutes already? I thought. *Time to head back in.*

Mom's Alzheimer's had been getting worse in the last few months. The more it affected her, the more she took it out on me. I knew it was her illness and not really her, but as her caregiver, I was directly in the line of fire.

The nurse arrived at 10am, as scheduled, and I took the opportunity to leave the apartment to take a couple of breaths outside to calm down. But as soon as I stepped out the door, the weight of everything became too much for me. I needed to decompress. I had to scream.

The faded green Bonneville belonged to my grandparents before they passed away a few years ago. I found comfort in the old car. What made it even more special was that I could put the windows up and release my frustrations without anyone hearing.

Screaming released all of my frustrations, but it always led to tears. I took another swipe at my tears with the back of my hand, then took a couple of deep breaths before checking the clock on the dashboard. *Yup, I had been gone for fifteen minutes. That was long enough, I needed to get back inside.*

As I entered the small apartment Mom and I shared, I was surprised to not see Mom or the nurse. The apartment was a one bedroom in a decent area east of Richmond. It had an oversized great room for ease of movement from the living room to the kitchen and vice versa. I expected to see them there. Instead, I was greeted with silence.

She must be helping her in the bath, I thought.

I dropped the keys into a crystal bowl that my mom won in a raffle years ago. The apartment was cluttered with all sorts of tchotchkes that she won at bingo and church raffles before she became too ill. The amount of things drove me crazy, but sometimes, even on bad days, Mom could find something that brought her some level of comfort, so I didn't touch them.

The keys clanked instead of the usual jingle they made in the bowl. I looked into the bowl and found something in there. It was about four inches long with a smiling skull looking up at me at one end. On the other end were two teeth.

It looked like it was made of glass so I carefully picked it up. The key was much heavier than I expected, especially for such a delicate material. It fit perfectly in the palm of my hand as I examined it.

I tried to think about all the things Mom had won but couldn't remember seeing anything like this skeleton key before. I definitely would have remembered seeing it. I wondered if Mom found it earlier and remembered anything from it.

Carrying the key towards the bathroom, I realized how quiet the apartment was. Something wasn't right. I didn't have to get where I was going, I knew Mom and the nurse weren't there.

I ran down the hall to my mother's room. As I pushed open the door, I saw my mother lying on her side, sleeping.

Not wanting to wake her, I turned around and walked back to the kitchen. On the counter was a note from the nurse.

Lilac,

I'm sorry, but I just got a call that I'm needed elsewhere in an emergency situation. Rose said she was feeling tired and went to her room to take a nap. I know you're right outside so I figured it was alright if I left. I'll be back tomorrow.

Mom didn't usually take naps. I couldn't shake the feeling that something was wrong. The key dropped from my hand onto the wooden kitchen floor and slid out of my sight.

"Shoot," I muttered.

I grabbed the broom, expecting the glass key to have shattered, but when I found it it was still in one piece. Even the delicate teeth were still in place.

As I picked it up, the thick glass looked blue, which was my mother's favorite color. I had this sudden strange feeling that I had to check on her. I rushed over to her bedroom and stepped inside.

She was still. Too still. The way she was lying down was exactly how she usually slept, but I knew she wasn't sleeping. I touched her arm and shook her gently.

"Mom? Please wake up, Mom," I whispered. I didn't need to check her pulse to know she was gone. I touched her face, which was still warm, but she didn't move. She wasn't breathing. She was gone.

CHAPTER 2

Three days later, I was parking the Bonneville at the same cemetery Mom and I had buried my grandparents at. The last few days were a blur, but I didn't mind.

It was a dreary and grey Saturday afternoon, the perfect day to bury my mother. The parking lot was empty except for a few cars. I didn't see anyone around. Wearing a black skirt, flats, and a simple short-sleeved black blouse, I stepped out of my car as a gust of wind whipped through me.

"Excuse me, Miss Martin," a raspy male voice said.

I turned towards the man as I wondered where he came from. I had been so numb lately that I barely knew what was going on around me.

The man had a slight build and wisps of grey hair. He was wearing a black suit that hung loosely on his thin frame.

"I see you found the key," he said.

I reached up and grabbed the glass skeleton key I now wore around my neck like a pendant. *Did I hear him right?* I had become attached to the key in the last few days. I imagined it being in the glass bowl because my mother wanted to show it to me. Maybe it meant something to her, I didn't know, but it now had meaning to me.

"Are you with the funeral home?" I asked.

"I've been waiting for you," he said

"We're ready for you, Miss Lilac," said a familiar voice from behind me.

I turned around and found Wyndham Bickle, the funeral director, walking towards me. I met him halfway, expecting the man who was talking to me to join us. But when I looked around for him, he was gone.

***

I sat on the small metal folding chair the funeral home set up beside the gravesite staring at the simple coffin in front of me. She would have hated that coffin. I remembered her showing me the ones with thick glossy wood and silk interiors when I was younger and telling me that was what she wanted to be buried in, but I couldn't afford that. This would join her list of ways I disappointed her.

Reminding myself of the few negative things about her was the only way I was able to get through the past few days. She was my best friend and confidant. I didn't know what I was going to do without her, but I knew I had to keep living.

She had followed me to Arizona twelve years ago while I earned my bachelors and masters degrees in Architecture. She didn't want me being so far from home so she decided if she couldn't convince me to stay, she would move too.

Shortly after her diagnosis, Mom told me she wanted to return to central Virginia. She found comfort in the tall trees and lakes where she had spent most of her life. She missed it and hoped being surrounded by all her memories would help. I would do anything to help her.

I left my job as an architect behind and got a job working in our local grocery store to make ends meet. It was the only way I had the flexibility to take her to her doctor appointments and make sure she was getting the best care possible.

Behind me, Wyndham cleared his throat. I ignored him. I maxed out my credit cards paying for everything for the funeral. He was probably ready to leave. I didn't care, he could leave if he wanted to, but I wasn't going anywhere just yet. He would have to pick me up and carry me away if he wanted me to go.

As the waft of his clean scent hit me, I planted my feet on the ground and wrapped my fingers around the edge of the seat.

"Excuse me, Miss Lilac," Wyndham said, his slight Southern accent coming through fuller when he pronounced my name. "I don't mean to rush you, but the cemetery folks are ready to lower the casket. They're only here for a limited time and--"

"Then let them lower it," I said.

"It's not customary."

"Trust me, I'm not going to throw myself onto her casket or anything. I just don't have anywhere else to go right now."

His right brow shot up as he eyed my face. He didn't like my answer, but I didn't care. Wyndham had acted fatherly since I first stepped foot into the funeral home. I didn't need it. I never knew my father, I didn't need some stranger acting like one now.

"Are you feeling alright?" he asked. "You look a little pale."

"That's normal for me. Can you please leave me alone now?"

My voice cracked and he looked at me with pity. I pushed my straight black hair behind my ear and looked away.

Pompous ass. I don't need your pity, I thought. *I have enough problems.*

Behind him, a few men in jeans shuffled their feet. They stood next to a covered pile of dirt, several shovels neatly stacked behind them.

Like covering it hides what the dirt is there for.

A corner of my mouth tugged up at the thought of anyone being gullible enough to not recognize a large mound of dirt. I covered my mouth with my hand and forced myself to keep a straight face.

Only a freak would start laughing at a funeral.

Wyndham shrugged and signaled to the men to pick up their shovels. He pressed a button near the grave that I hadn't seen before and a quiet motor turned on.

I picked up the bouquet of bright yellow daisies, Mom's favorite, from my lap as I stood. As the casket began its slow descent into the ground, I tossed the flowers on top.

I spent the past five years helping my mother as she struggled with Alzheimer's. Now that she was gone, knowing that she was finally at peace, I didn't know what to do with myself. I had no one else to worry about but myself. I didn't know how to do that.

As much as I didn't want to look at it, my eyes were drawn to the gravestone. Our family name, Martin, was carved boldly across most of the stone. Underneath was what I didn't want to see--my grandparents' names with their birth and death dates. The funeral home assured me my mother's name would be added soon.

As I looked at my grandparents' names, Lilac and John, I realized I should have brought something for them too. I always brought them gifts to their graves on their birthdays. I should have brought them something now.

Remembering something my grandmother used to do, I knelt in the grass. As I moved my hands over its thick, cool blades, I found what I was looking for. I dug my fingers into the earth and pulled up a stone, brushed it off, and placed it on the headstone.

"I miss you," I whispered to my grandparents. "And Mom, try to behave yourself."

As I said goodbye, I realized the only thing left for me in Virginia were my memories.

"Are you sure you're alright?" Wyndham asked as I turned away from the grave and returned to my seat.

His brown eyes looked sad, and I could tell it wasn't just part of his job. He was genuinely concerned.

"I'll be fine," I said. "I just have a lot of things to figure out."

"Do you have any friends or family you can visit? Maybe it would help if you spent some time away."

"No, I have some friends back in Arizona, but that's about it. This is where my family is now. Plus I don't have the money to go anywhere."

I looked back at the grave as he nodded.

"I imagine you haven't had much time to socialize the past five years you've been back," he said.

"I haven't. And now I need to figure out what to do with myself."

"You'll be fine," he said. "I'm sure of it."

He patted me on my shoulder before walking away.

I sat back on the folding chair as the men shoveled dirt over my mother's coffin. I didn't know what to do with myself. I never thought this day would actually come, and I hated myself for feeling relief from it.

I had my life back. I was thirty-two and could do anything I wanted, but I was too numb to think. I wanted to get back to my career and restore historic buildings, but how could I? Who would even hire me when my sabbatical was longer than the two years experience I had?

The sky darkened over the tall trees surrounding the cemetery. The last thing I wanted was to be stuck in a downpour, no matter how fitting it was. It was time for me to go.

As I walked back to the green Bonneville, I heard footsteps behind me. I didn't turn around. I kept my eyes on the car and kept walking towards it. They had all my money, they didn't need anything else from me.

The footsteps quickened as they came closer. The tiny hairs at the back of my neck stood. My heart raced. Why was I acting like this? What was going on? Thick black clouds moved overhead. As I got closer to the car, I put my hand out towards the door, ready to jump in. I was shaking.

A gust of wind whipped past me, taking my breath away. As I gasped for air, I spun around, expecting to see whoever was behind me, but no one was there.

I turned back towards the car and the man from earlier appeared out of nowhere.

"Jeez!" I exclaimed, taking a step back from him with my trembling hand over my pounding heart.

"Pardon me, Miss Martin," he said. "I didn't mean to frighten you. I was hoping to speak to you before you left."

His voice had a calming lilt to it as if he was singing a lullaby, but there was an underlying tone that said he was lying. He meant to scare me and he enjoyed doing it. He grinned, revealing large perfect teeth behind his chapped lips.

"You didn't frighten me," I lied. "Are you with the funeral home?"

"Who I am is unimportant, but who I represent is. I am Julien Lambert's attaché."

His eyebrow cocked up as if he was expecting me to be impressed. I wasn't. I didn't know who Julien Lambert was or why I should care.

"So?" I asked.

The moist air stood still, clinging to me like a wet blanket. I wanted to get into the Bonneville and blast the air, but I couldn't help but be curious about this man.

His eyes flashed with annoyance before his features relaxed into a patronizing grin.

"My dear, surely you have heard of Chateau du Soleil."

"Of course I have. Anyone who grew up in central Virginia knows about Chateau du Soleil," I said, not admitting I was obsessed with the place.

"Well then you should know that Julien Lambert is the owner."

"Someone owns it?" I asked, surprised.

Chateau du Soleil was the reason I specialized in Historic Restoration for my master's degree. I always dreamed that one day I would see it from the inside. I was shocked to hear it had an owner. As far as I knew, it had been abandoned long before I was born.

"Of course someone owns it," he scoffed, then looked up at the sky as the clouds began to break. He reached into his pocket and pulled out a business card and held it out to me. "I must be going, but here's my card. I'll cut to the chase--Mr. Lambert wants you to repair Chateau du Soleil. He is familiar with your work and is offering for you to move in with the expectation that you will focus on this project and only this project."

"Wait, what?" I couldn't have heard him right. "You want me to restore Chateau du Soleil?"

He pursed his lips as his brow wrinkled with annoyance.

"That *is* what I said, miss." He spoke slowly, carefully enunciating each word as if he believed I had no ability to understand him.

"And this *is* my mother's funeral," I said, speaking just as slowly. "Only an asshole would track someone down at a funeral to talk about work."

He stared into the cemetery with a dumbfounded expression. Restoring the castle would be a dream come true, but why track me down here? It had to be some kind of scam or a joke.

As I opened the car door, his hand slammed against the window, closing it.

"You'd be a fool to let this slip by. You have the key, you were meant for this. I would give anything for the chance. I would do anything for him," he said.

His words were quick but hushed. His eyes darted back and forth with a mixture of suspicion and paranoia. He shoved the business card in my hand.

"It is your choice," he said. "Just know that the offer stands as it is."

He walked backwards, his eyes still locked on me. The wind picked up again, making me shiver. I jumped into the car as I looked for the man again, but he was gone.

"What was he talking about? Just my luck that the crazies always find me," I said to myself.

I turned the car on and started to drive, not caring where I was going. I was too numb to think, too tired to care. I let the road lead the way.

CHAPTER 3

I drove on autopilot to the apartment Mom and I shared until a couple of days ago. As I pulled the car into a parking spot near the building, I realized I still had the business card in my hand.

It was a plain white business card with small black lettering centered on one side and nothing on the other. To my surprise, the name was Julien Lambert and not the weirdo who was at the cemetery. The offer was too good to be true and the man sounded so crazy, I didn't think I could believe him, but I wanted to. Restoring the castle would be a dream come true.

As I got out of the car, the sky finally opened up. Rain pelted my skin as I walked to the small porch. I always liked the rain.

I entered the apartment and dropped my keys into the crystal bowl by the door before heading to my bedroom. Intending on changing clothes, I grabbed an old grey sweatshirt I had from a trip Mom and I had taken to Williamsburg years ago, but got distracted by an old photo. Everything around me reminded me of Mom, and I took comfort in it.

The photo reminded me of Mom's old photo albums. I grabbed an old one she kept in the living room and set it on an end table. When I wasn't thinking about Mom, my mind turned to Chateau du Soleil. Sitting on the old tweed couch with my legs tucked under me, I pulled the business card out again.

Could this be for real?

I flipped it over, held it up to the light, and then bent it between my thumb and middle finger, looking for an answer. None came. The kitchen phone rang, startling me, and I jumped up to grab it before I had to hear the loud piercing tone again.

"Hello?" I answered, my voice hoarse.

"Lilac? Are you sick?" Robin asked.

Robin was one of the few friends I still had. We met in college and tried to talk on the phone a couple of times a week now that I was so far away.

I cleared my throat. I lost my voice momentarily whenever I was surprised.

"No, it's nothing," I said. "You know we have this old-fashioned rotary phone. Damn thing scared the crap out of me."

"Ahh, that explains it. How'd it go today?"

"Weird. I don't know. I wish you could've flown out here."

"I know, me too. I really wanted to be there for you. You know I loved your mom."

"She loved you too. You were one of the few people she seemed to remember properly. I know you would've been here if you could have, but I was fine on my own anyway."

"You sure? I know you and I know you say you're fine when you're really not," she said.

I sighed and closed my eyes for a second before shaking my head.

"You're shaking your head, aren't you?" she asked.

"I am. You're right, I'm not okay. I just feel so guilty. Like maybe I didn't do enough, maybe I should have done things differently."

"You did the best you could. I know it was tough especially the last year or so, but you did everything you could. Your mom would've been proud of everything you did for her if things were different."

I shook my head.

"You're doing it again, aren't you?" she asked. "You're shaking your head."

"I am."

Robin couldn't really understand, she didn't know everything that happened. Mom made it clear that she wasn't proud of me. She reminded me of how much of a disappointment I was to her. I couldn't tell Robin that, I couldn't tell anyone. I knew it was her illness talking, but it didn't make it sting any less.

"Don't be so hard on yourself, Lilac. You know your mom loved you."

"Maybe," I said, deciding it was time to change the subject. "I sometimes wonder if she *really* didn't like me. She did name me Lilac."

Robin laughed. "She named you after her mom."

"Obviously. I just wish Grandma didn't have such a silly name." It felt good to laugh. I couldn't remember the last time I had. Stretching the phone cord as far as it would go, I sat on the couch and picked up the business card again. "Oh hey, you've got to hear this. So I was walking to my car and this freak comes up to me."

"You've got to kidding me. I'm telling you, men hit on you everywhere. I bet it's those high cheekbones and warm brown eyes."

"Nooooo, no, it wasn't like that at all. I'm pretty sure this guy escaped from the loony bin and if it wasn't for what he was offering, I would have thrown the card away. Remember I told you about that castle, Chateau du Soleil? They want me to renovate it."

"No way, how'd that happen?" she asked.

"I have no idea. I've barely done anything and I've spent the past five years working at the grocery store, but he claims the owner knows my work."

"You think it's a scam, don't you?"

"What else could it be?" I asked. "I barely got started on my career when Mom got sick. Just seems like a lot of work to find out about me and track me down at my mother's funeral."

"Not to mention rude."

"Exactly. I mean, who would do that?"

"But you're still thinking about calling? Just in case it is real, right?"

I chewed my lip while I thought about that. This was Chateau du Soleil. If I ignored it and it turned out to be the real thing, then I'd never forgive myself. Slowly, I started nodding.

"You're nodding, aren't you?" Robin said.

"I am. I'm going to call the owner. I'll call you back if I find out anything."

"You'd better."

I got up and placed the phone back on its cradle on the kitchen wall, then picked up my cell phone and started dialing. The phone rang three times and I quickly looked at the business card to make sure I dialed the right number. I did. After the fifth ring, I heard a click and then silence.

Did someone pick it up? Maybe I didn't hear them answer.

"Umm…hello?" I asked, unsure if someone was there or if I got disconnected.

A breath caught on the other end and then there was more silence.

"Is someone there?" I asked nervously. "I…umm…was given this business card by…" That jackass didn't give me his name! "The…uhh… attaché to Julien Lambert--"

"Lam-BERT?" he scoffed, interrupting me. "You silly Americans destroy every beautiful language. It's pronounced Lam-BEAR."

"Oh. I'm sorry, I didn't know." I wracked my brain trying to remember how the man this afternoon pronounced the name, but I couldn't remember. "I didn't mean any disrespect."

"And who are you?" he asked.

"Lilac Martin. I was told--"

"Ahh, the architect. Dinner is in an hour. It is in your best interest to attend."

The line went dead and I stood, still in the kitchen, staring at the phone in my palm. I didn't have time to change or even think. If I wanted this job, I had to get to the castle within the hour.

CHAPTER 4

Even though they were expecting me, I was still skeptical about the offer. The chateau faced the James River, giving it an incredible view. The gravel driveway ended at the side of the castle, in an alcove between two tall turrets.

As I stepped out of the car, I realized I had no idea how to get into the building. Worried I would twist my ankle and end up embarrassing myself, I took small careful steps on the gravel. I remembered in the fall when the trees were bare, the front of the chateau was visible from the road. I just needed to figure out which direction that was.

A tall thin man in a bright blue suit came running through the grass. His black hair was slicked back from his forehead and he had an air of seriousness about him. I couldn't imagine him ever telling a joke.

"We've been waiting for you, mademoiselle," he said with a thick French accent. "Dinner will be served in five minutes. You do not want to disappoint Monsieur Lambert."

With how he pronounced Lambert, I knew this was the man who answered the phone earlier.

"I'm sorry, I got here as fast as I could," I said.

As I approached, his eyes wandered up and down over my outfit. He frowned and shook his head disapprovingly.

"That's what you chose to wear? You look like you just came from a funeral."

"Actually, I did."

His cheeks flushed for a moment as his eyes widened.

"Oh, my deepest apologies," he said. "I forgot where Hugo said he contacted you."

"Hugo? The weird man at the cemetery?"

To my surprise, he chuckled softly before sweeping his arm towards the front of the chateau.

"Hugo is…shall we say intense?" His hazel eyes twinkled and I realized I read him wrong before. "We don't get out much, so please forgive my manners. I am Alexander, Monsieur Lambert's butler."

Chateau du Soleil was a light grey brick neo-gothic building with six tall pointed turrets and an oversized iron double door entry. The combination of the turrets with the gothic architecture made the chateau look like it belonged in a fairy tale.

The windows were tall and thin, similar to the churches of the time period. The turrets were dark, almost black, and reminded me of witches's hats. The castle was even more beautiful up close than I ever imagined, even if it was in disrepair.

As we entered the chateau, I didn't know where to look first. The main hall had a brown and beige Spanish mosaic tile floor, wood-beamed ceiling with iron accents, and three large but simple chandeliers. Across from the entry was a large curved staircase with red carpeting that led to a balcony overlooking the entry. The main wings had tall archways before the carpeted halls. Lastly, all the keyhole doorways had thick wooden spiral molding along the sides.

It was easy for me to look past the broken and missing tile, the cracked walls, and torn carpeting. The chateau had so much potential to be beautiful again. It just needed a little love.

A woman with her grey hair swept up into a bun and a large white apron over her sky blue dress ran over to us. Her brown eyes were filled with concern and she wrung her hands together as she turned and looked towards the large archway she came out of.

"What is it, Elyse?" Alexander asked.

"He is--" she said before getting interrupted by a loud crash down the hall she had emerged from, "in a bad mood."

"Does he know?" he asked.

"No, I just told him it was time for dinner."

"Good, he'll come. Is everything set?"

"Yes." She turned to me and smiled sweetly. "We're delighted to have you, miss. We don't get many visitors. I hope you're hungry, I made my specialty."

She hurried off before I could answer. Alexander cleared his throat and looked down the hall with apprehension before taking a step in that direction.

"This way please," he said. "I'll show you to the dining room."

The chateau looked worn, but not in too bad shape. The walls were stone with some rugs hanging to give the place warmth. The floor was constructed of tiny tiles in a herringbone pattern. There were cracks in the walls and some missing tiles, but for a castle that had been transported and rebuilt centuries ago and then not lived in, I expected it to look worse.

Alexander stopped at a doorway and extended his arm, signaling me to enter the room. The dining room had a long wooden table in the center. Above it dangled a candle chandelier that was the only source of light in the room. Three ceiling-to-floor stained glass windows of purple flowers drew my attention. They were reminiscent of Tiffany glass windows from the 19th century and as I got closer to them, I realized the flowers were lilacs.

"These are incredible," I said.

"Ahh yes, they are. Monsieur Lambert had them installed after Chateau du Soleil was rebuilt."

"After it was rebuilt? Do you mean this has been in the family for all these years?"

Alexander looked away nervously.

"*Oui*, that is exactly what I meant," he said. "Let me show you to your seat."

He pulled a heavy wooden chair with a thick leather seat out for me. As I sat down, he pushed the chair in. Stomping feet echoed from the hall.

"Ahh, here comes Julien now," Alexander whispered.

"Dinner? You want me to sit for dinner?" Julien's voice was deep and boomed through the dining room as he entered wearing a pair of dark jeans and a crisp white button-down shirt. Elyse followed, looking frantic behind him.

"Sir, we have a guest," she said.

Her eyes widened and darted in my direction. His eyes followed and when our eyes met, my breath caught in my throat. Without realizing what I was doing, I stood from my seat and walked towards him.

His long legs cut across the room quickly. As he reached me, I thought he was going to take me into his arms, but instead he took a step back and stared at me intensely.

He was easily over six feet tall. His eyes were an icy blue, almost like they didn't have any color in them. With his wavy dark hair that brushed the tops of his shoulders, his skin looked paler than anyone I had seen before. He had a tight beard, an aristocratic nose, a dimple on his chin, and lips that curled up as he looked at me.

Julien was devilishly handsome, but the reason I reacted how I did was because he had the familiarity of someone I knew. I had never met him before, but I felt like I knew him intimately.

"What is she doing here?"

His eyes were still locked on mine, but then slowly drifted down to my neck.

"I haven't seen this in..." He shook his head in disbelief. "Where did you find this?" He reached for the skeleton key still hanging from a chain around my neck. "I must have it."

I jerked away and took a step back.

"Over my dead body," I said.

He laughed as he lowered his head and his eyes bore into me.

"That can be arranged," he said.

He smiled, revealing sharp points on two of his teeth.

CHAPTER 5

I stepped back from him. I couldn't take my eyes away from his teeth. Suddenly his skin wasn't just pale anymore, but deathly. Could he be a vampire? I was crazy just for thinking it.

The thought of running from him or screaming for help never crossed my mind. The familiarity I felt for him also told me I could trust him.

He moved closer to me and I punched him in the chest.

"Stop it! You're not going to bully me into giving you this key," I said.

His expression softened and I couldn't see the pointed teeth anymore.

"Oh, you'll give me the key," he said confidently. "No one ever denies me what I want."

"Well then you better prepare yourself for disappointment."

He laughed then turned from me and with his hands behind his back, he looked at the food Elyse had spread out on the table, then back at me.

"Please sit, join me for dinner. That's why you're here for anyway. We can discuss the key later while I show you around my home."

"No," I said as I folded my arms in front of me. "I'm not joining you for dinner. You obviously take pleasure in screwing with people's minds. You want me to think you're a vampire, don't you? I don't understand it, but I have a feeling you're not going to explain it."

He looked back at me and grinned slyly as he nodded.

For a moment I thought about leaving Chateau du Soleil and letting my dream go, but then I decided I shouldn't have to do that just because the owner was a strange jerk.

"Maybe you'll change your mind after a bite to eat," he said.

"I don't think so. Actually if you don't mind, I'd like to take the tour now and get to work right away."

His eyes darkened and his jaw clenched angrily.

"Fine," he said before turning to Alexander. "Show her around, then take her to her room." He turned back to me. "It is late. You'll be spending the night here. I will arrange for all of your things to be packed in the morning."

"No," I said. "I'm not going to let strangers pack my things."

The thought of movers coming and pack all my mother's belongings made me smile. I wasn't ready to deal with all the emotions I had from losing her, but every day became easier.

"Fine, then I'll leave it to you to arrange everything," he said. "Remember you are free to come and go as you please, but I expect regular updates on your progress. Now if you don't mind, I have more pressing matters."

He walked out of the dining room and his boots echoed in the hall. Elyse disappeared through another door and Alexander cleared his throat as he approached me.

"That went better than I expected," he said.

"Why didn't you warn me?" I asked.

"Would you have stayed if I explained you would be working for a vampire?"

My heart stopped for a moment as his words sank into my brain.

"But how can that be?" I asked.

"That is up to him to tell." He pulled my chair out and waved at the food on the table. "Elyse prepared all of this for you. Would you like a bite before I show you around?"

I finally focused on the food she had set out. There were five different plates, and each one had a different food that I loved.

"How did she know?" I asked.

"There's not much about you we don't know, mademoiselle." He smiled warmly. "You've had a long day. Please enjoy your meal and when you're done, I'll give you the tour."

"Just one quick question," I said, then waited for him to nod before I continued. "Are you, Hugo, and Elysa..." Unable to say the word, my voice trailed off.

"Vampires?" he scoffed. "No."

"Wait, so then--" *How are you still alive?*

"No, you said one question, I've let you have several," he said.

"But--"

"Please, Lilac, give it time," Alexander said, his voice gentle. "Everything will be clear soon."

***

After my meal, Alexander showed me the rest of the wing, then we walked across the main hall to the other side of the castle. I had so many questions, but I knew asking Alexander would be a waste of time. He would never tell me what I wanted to know.

Many of the rooms had the furnishings covered. I guessed they lived in several rooms and didn't bother touching the others. I would have to take more time in the morning going through these rooms, but everything looked well-kept for a building that had been rebuilt over two centuries ago.

As Alexander walked me to my room, he pointed to a wide curving staircase with red carpeting.

"Monsieur Lambert has requested that you not go upstairs. He declared it off limits."

"Well then how does Mr. Lam-Bert expect me to complete the restoration?"

Alexander sighed.

"Lam-Bear. Say it, Lam-Bear."

"Lam-Bert," I said.

He shook his head, but dropped it while I smiled triumphantly.

I entered my room and was surprised by how elegant it was. In the center was an antique mahogany bed with thick winding bedposts. On top of the bedposts was an iron crown canopy that was open to the ceiling. The tall windows matched those in the dining room with the Tiffany glass lilacs. I patted the bed with my hand and it sank into the plush mattress.

"Wow, this is nice," I said.

I climbed on and lay flat on my back. The ceiling was painted like the night sky with stars. I loved it. I stared at the ceiling and picked out several constellations. But while I enjoyed the room and was tired enough to sleep, I couldn't help but wonder what rooms were at the top of the stairs.

Was that where Julien slept? Did this castle have a dungeon? Maybe a vampire would like that better.

I got up and went to the door and looked out into the hall. I listened, trying to hear if anyone was around, but there was only silence.

I closed the bedroom door behind me and quickly made my way down the hall to the main hall. Before stepping out of the archway, I peeked at the entrance, but no one was around.

Unsure if any of the steps would squeak from age, I chose my footing carefully. When I reached the top of the stairs, there was only one hall to go down. It was lit with candle wall sconces, but bright enough for me to see where I was going.

I tried several doors and entered those rooms, but none of them gave me any clue as to why I shouldn't be in this section of the house.

Just as I was about to give up, I noticed a painting at the end of the hall. It was too dark to make out what it was so I grabbed my cell phone and turned on the flashlight.

"Oh my," I whispered as my eyes adjusted.

In front of me was a wall-sized oil painting that looked like me, but in a Victorian era dress. It was a purple- and cream-colored dress with short ruffled sleeves, fitted bodice, and a full skirt. I had never seen that dress before, but I knew it was made of silk and felt soft and airy.

I was so stunned by the painting that my phone slipped out of my hand. As I bent to pick it up from the floor, my elbow hit the painting and made a soft thud.

"Wait a second," I whispered. "That doesn't sound right."

I thought about where I was in the house but was so turned around I couldn't figure it out. Grabbing the edge of the painting, I pulled it a little with one hand while using my flashlight in the other. The painting didn't move like it was attached to the wall.

Pulling hard, the painting creaked as it moved on hinges. I moved back as I pushed it open more, then aimed my light at the wall behind it.

In front of me was a large wooden door with intricate carvings. I ran my fingers over them as I examined them. I thought they were telling a story, but without enough light, I couldn't see enough to piece it together.

As my hand traveled down the door, I reached the iron doorknob. I twisted it, trying to force it open, but it didn't budge.

It must be rusted. I thought. *Or it's locked.*

I reached for the heavy glass key around my neck.

Stranger things had happened today. Maybe this will open the door.

I removed it from my necklace. My hands were trembling as I moved it closer to the lock.

There's something behind this door. This is what he doesn't want me to see, I thought.

"What do you think you're doing?" Julien demanded.

CHAPTER 6

I jumped at the sound of Julien's voice. Spinning around to face him, I closed my hand around the key.

"Nothing. I got lost," I said.

His eyes narrowed as he scanned my face. I forced myself to stay calm and not act as guilty as I felt.

"You're not supposed to be up here," he growled. "I'm sure Alexander told you it's dangerous."

"It doesn't look dangerous to me, other than being a little dark."

"You haven't changed a bit," he muttered as he turned away from me.

"Is that good or bad?" I asked.

He glanced back at me as the corners of his lips tugged upwards.

"It's good. Very good."

As he started to walk away, I pushed the painting back into place and turned on my cell phone's flashlight.

"Can you tell me about this?" I asked.

He stopped and looked at the painting for a moment as his smile deepened.

"I can tell you it needs a better spotlight," he said before continuing down the hall.

"No, Julien, wait. Please answer me."

"I can't," he said before he disappeared into the darkness.

I turned back and looked at the painting again. I had to find out what was on the other side of that door.

Squinting, I looked down the dark hall, hoping to see if I was alone or not, but it was too dark to tell. I gave up and headed back to my room with a plan to come back later that night.

*****

As I lay in bed looking at the ceiling, questions filled my mind about Julien, the door, and the people working for him. So much had happened today that I started to question if I was dreaming.

Logic told me I was probably exhausted and still grieving for my mom. Both of those were true, but did it mean I was making things up? I didn't think so and I wanted to learn more.

I quickly traced my route back to the painting and the locked wooden door behind it. I prepared myself for disappointment as I moved the key closer to the keyhole. What were the chances it would work? And even if it did, would it matter? Anything could be on the other side of that door.

The key slid into the lock like it had a mind of its own. I slowly reached out for the doorknob and turned it. The door was unlocked!

I was so surprised that the skeleton key worked that I stood holding the twisted doorknob without pulling the door open. Just as I was ready to find out what was on the other side of the door, I thought to pull the key out and put it in my pocket. Then, with a big breath, I opened the door.

I expected to see another room in the castle, but it was gone. On the other side of the door, dark fog followed the occasional gusts of wind.

I had no fear. All I could think about were the years I spent taking care of my mom, and now she was gone. I needed to do something wild, something that wasn't in character for me. I had to move forward with my life and accept that she was at peace.

I stepped forward and a gust of wind whipped around me. As it died down, I realized I was outside of Chateau du Soleil, but I wasn't in Virginia anymore.

A horse-drawn carriage sped past me to the entrance. The castle glowed as people entered the main hall for a party. As I stepped forward, my clothes made a loud swish. I looked at myself and realized I was in the purple dress from the painting. Reaching up, I discovered my hair was pulled up with a jeweled comb.

I was in awe as I entered the main hall. Chateau du Soleil looked like it did in my dreams. I didn't understand how it happened, but somehow that door took me into the past.

Remembering that I placed the skeleton key in a pocket that I wasn't wearing anymore, I patted myself, trying to feel the thick glass of the key as my heart raced. What if I lost the key? How would I get back? What if I couldn't find the door?

Suddenly my hand brushed against something hard. I ran my hand over the sleek silk until I found a hidden pocket and pulled out the key. As I breathed a sigh of relief, I stepped farther into the main hall.

Alexander clicked his heels and lowered his head towards me in greeting. *How could he be here?* I pushed my confusion aside and reminded myself that even though I knew him, he didn't know I shouldn't be there. My time hadn't happened yet. He smiled broadly as he approached.

"Good evening, mademoiselle," he said. "He's been waiting for you."

I nodded and followed the crowd up the steps into the wing I was told to not enter. Instead of being dark, it was brightly lit. As I walked with the other guests, I realized we were going to the end of the hall, to the door I used the key on.

Expecting to see the carved wooden door at the end of the hall, I was surprised to find an open archway that led to a ballroom. As I entered, my eyes swept up to the glittering chandeliers and gold finishing on the ornate ceiling.

The guests continued to enter the room while I stood in awe. I had never seen anything so extravagant before. The slim glass windows that surrounded the ballroom reflected the candlelight. In a corner, five men sat holding their violins as they waited for a signal. The center of the ballroom was empty except for the people milling about.

A warm hand softly touched my back before lips whispered into my ear.

"You're late, as usual," Julien said. "One day I'll learn to tell you to arrive an hour earlier than I'm expecting."

I turned to him, and he took my hand and bowed deeply as he kissed it. He was wearing a cream-colored suit made out of the same silk as my dress. His eyes were the color of the sea, not the icy blue of the vampire I met.

"Come, everyone's been waiting for us to have our first dance," he said.

"First dance?" I asked.

"Yes, you know it's customary. Plus I've been waiting for our first dance as a betrothed couple. Like I said, you're late," he teased.

He signaled the violins and they began to play. Still holding my hand, he raised it as he led me to the middle of the dance floor. With a wave of his arm, he bowed to me and the crowd applauded.

I was overwhelmed and stunned. Not only had I known Julien, but he was my fiancé. It didn't explain why he felt so familiar to me, but as he took me into his arms and we waltzed, I was willing to believe anything.

As we moved around the dance floor, Julien's gaze was locked onto mine. It made everything and everyone vanish. It was just us, together. He smiled and his entire face lit up. I could tell he loved me and something unexplainable deep inside of me, like a memory, loved him too.

"It feels like an eternity since I've seen you," he whispered into my ear. "Let's get some air on the balcony."

I nodded, and he led me off the dance floor as other couples took our place.

A hunched-over elderly woman dressed in black tugged on Julien's sleeve.

"Excuse me, Monsieur Lambert," she said. "It would brighten my soul if you agreed to a dance with me."

Julien stopped and smiled at the woman. "I would be honored, but perhaps later."

We continued towards the open stained glass doors of the balcony, but she tugged on his sleeve again.

"I'm only asking for a dance," she said. "Just a few moments of your time."

He looked torn for a moment before he spoke. "Do you see this beautiful woman here?" he asked the woman. "She has promised to be mine for as long as we both live. This is our first time together as a betrothed couple, so please allow me to steal some moments with her."

The woman's face turned red and she shook her fist at us.

"You'll pay for this," she said before hobbling away and disappearing into the crowd.

I felt bad for her for being so upset, but he never told her no. Julien shrugged and as we finally reached the balcony, he pressed his lips against mine and pulled me close against him.

His kiss made me dizzy and I finally understood the phrase "weak at the knees." As his lips left mine, I kept my eyes closed and replayed the kiss in my mind.

"I love you, Lilac," he whispered.

I opened my eyes and confusion set in. The ceiling was painted with stars. I sat up in bed and discovered I was still in my clothing from the funeral the day before.

"Please don't tell me that was just a dream," I said as I rubbed my eyes. "It felt so real."

Beside me, on the bed, lay the skeleton key. Was it there because I fell asleep or because I used it? I was so confused I didn't know what was real anymore.

Then, as I ran my fingers through my hair, a jeweled hair comb fell onto the bed.

That was real! But how?

CHAPTER 7

Sitting in the dining room, I sketched my ideas for the restoration. After seeing the chateau three nights ago, I knew exactly what needed to be done to bring it back to its former glory.

Alexander arranged for movers to pack my apartment and bring everything to Chateau du Soleil. I was grateful I didn't have to pack everything myself. I didn't want to deal with all of my mother's things. Packing them up would feel like losing her all over again.

I met the movers at the apartment the day after my dinner at the chateau. I packed all of my personal belongings and they took care of the rest. It was sad seeing all of my mom's things being packed away, but I needed to move forward and not dwell like I sometimes did.

The suite next to my bedroom became my storage room. Everything from the apartment was being kept in there. I liked having it so close, it made it easy to access if I decided I needed something.

In the meanwhile, I had made myself at home there. I enjoyed my time researching the history of the building and drawing my sketches.

Since I was alone, I pulled out my cell phone to update Robin. I had spoken to her the other day while I packed and she didn't seem very happy. I tried probing for what was bothering her, but she ended the call quickly.

As I waited for Robin to pick up her phone, I heard Julien's heavy footsteps in the hall. Robin's voicemail answered so I hung up. I would try her again another time.

"Did you enjoy yourself the other night?" Julien asked as he entered the room.

"The other night?" I asked innocently.

I slid my sketch of the ballroom underneath the others then started shading in the staircase in the main hall. There was no way he could know about what happened and I wasn't going to tell him.

"Don't play dumb, it's unbecoming," he said.

He pulled out the chair next to mine, sat down, and looked at my sketches. I pulled them back and straightened the pile.

"They're not ready for you to see yet," I said. "I sketch while I'm putting together my ideas."

"Just let me see one," he said.

"Just one?"

"Yes, but I get to pick."

"Okay, which room do you want to see?" I asked as I set my pencil down.

"The ballroom."

"Oh? There's a ballroom here?"

I picked up my pencil again and went back to shading the staircase, careful to not look at him.

"You have no idea how well I know you," he said as one corner of his mouth tugged upwards.

It was the first time I had seen him with a sly half smile, but I knew what it meant. He caught me. I didn't know how, but he knew.

I looked up and met his gaze.

"How did that happen?" I asked. "How did I go back?"

"You know why. You saw what happened." He gritted his teeth and a darkness spread across his pale blue eyes. "Just promise you won't go back. Give me that skeleton key so I can destroy it."

"I know what I saw, but it still doesn't explain anything." I ignored what he said about the key. I wasn't going to give it to him.

"We're meant to be together, ma chérie. We promised to spend our lives together and that didn't happen. Not yet at least."

"What do you mean?"

"Why do you think you're here? Do you really think you're only here for the chateau? I knew you would come back. I moved the chateau here to get away from my memories in France, but I can't escape some of them. I've been waiting for you," he said. "And like always, you are late."

"Be serious. I don't understand what's going on. You've been alive for two hundred years. I need more than a few days to accept all of this."

"I'm sorry, you're right. This is why I didn't seek you out," he said. "I knew you would eventually come back, but you don't need this life. You don't need to be trapped here."

"What do you mean trapped?" I thought about Alexander being in the past. Then I thought about that first day when he said Hugo didn't get out much. I thought it was a joke, but maybe there was a lot more truth to it. "Are they all vampires?"

"No," he said quietly. "Just me. But they're tied to the castle, just as you are. Out of love."

"You don't want me here?" I asked.

"I do. Every day, something reminds me of you. But after what happened," he shook his head sadly. "I can't bear the thought of losing you again. I didn't want you to come here, but Elyse, Hugo, and Alexander had a different plan."

"And now that I'm here?"

"Now I don't want you to leave." He took my hand and pressed it to his cold lips. "Promise me you won't go back to the door. I don't know how you got that key, but it must be destroyed. It's too dangerous."

"Why?"

"Just listen to me. Trust me," he said.

I nodded, and he got up and left the room. I did trust him, but for the past three days all I had thought about was going back. I wanted to dance with him again. I wanted the castle to be beautiful. I wanted to feel his love again.

As I pulled my ballroom sketch out from under the others, a sketch of Julien in the past slipped out of the stack. I couldn't help myself, I kept thinking about him. I thought about that kiss, about the warmth of his hand, and how happy I felt when I was with him. I realized that no matter what he said, I had to go back. I needed to experience our past again.

***

I meant to try the door earlier in the evening, but time slipped away from me after I returned to my room. I must have been more tired than I realized because I woke up to the grandfather clock in the main hall chiming three times.

I stretched and got out of bed still dressed, then grabbed the key. As I opened the door to the bedroom, I looked down the hall to make sure I was alone again. With no one around, I quickly made my way to the other wing.

Being more familiar with the dark wing, I was able to make my way to the end of the hall quicker than the other night. As soon as I reached the painting, I yanked it open, excited to get back through the door. I knew I was acting a little careless, but all I could think about was getting back to the past and seeing Julien again.

I put the key in the door and turned the knob, expecting to find myself at the same party as I had three nights ago. Instead I was surrounded by a thick fog and when it cleared, I found myself in the middle of the woods just beyond the castle.

Chateau du Soleil glowed in the distance. The sky was darker than it was when I was there the other night. I remembered seeing a clear night sky, but this one was threatening.

Clouds rolled in as a storm thundered over the mountains. Ahead of me, I heard the sound of horse-drawn carriages arriving at the chateau. I followed the sound knowing it would bring me to the entrance.

I walked carefully through the woods in the silk slippers I wore three nights before. The skirt of my long dress caught on a branch, making me jump. I swiped it away from the bush before continuing forward towards the chateau. As I reached the edge of the forest, I realized I was on the other side of the castle underneath the ballroom.

Movement on the balcony caught my eye. Looking up, I tried to see if it was Julien and I, but all I saw was Julien heading back into the ballroom alone. I wondered what happened to me. *Where did past me go?* I walked towards the front of the castle, intent on finding him, when something made a loud noise in the woods behind me.

A tall muscular man stepped out of the woods wearing a black suit with a long coat. His platinum-colored hair was wild and fell past his shoulders. He leered at me as his lips shifted into an ugly smirk. Everything in my body told me to run as fast as I could, but I knew that even at my fastest, I wasn't going to be fast enough.

"Mother always finds the best treats for me," he said with a thick Russian accent.

His words sent ice through my veins. I backed away from him as he stepped closer. He widened his mouth into a smile and revealed sharp teeth. While it reminded me of Julien and the night he bared his fangs when I first arrived at the chateau, this was different. Tonight I felt fear.

"Treat?" I asked hesitantly. "What are you talking about?"

"She heard about your party tonight. All she wanted to do was dance with the future groom, but he turned her down."

His tone was so lighthearted I wasn't sure if I should take him seriously.

"He didn't turn her down," I said. "He told her he would dance with her later. I had just gotten here and he wanted to spend some time with me."

The woods echoed with his laughter. His smile widened menacingly as he stepped closer. I felt my gag reflex react as the scent of death drifted towards me.

"You seem to think I care about what happened. Let me tell you a little secret. I don't," he said. "All that matters to me is having my nightly meal. Mother can be...how do I say? A little self-centered and manipulative, but ultimately she answers to me."

His long pale fingers reached towards me and I jerked away.

"I am a man who always gets what I want, pretty thing," he said. "And right now I'm hungry."

I spun around and ran towards the castle. Behind me, the vampire laughed. He didn't chase me. He didn't have to. He had the unfair advantage of not being human. As I reached the clearing closest to the chateau's entrance, he appeared in front of me. I forced myself to stop so I wouldn't run into him. My slippers shifted in the wet grass, causing me to fall.

"I love it when they run away," he said. "You will definitely make a tasty morsel."

CHAPTER 8

The vampire leapt towards me, but I quickly rolled out of the way. I scrambled to my feet, but the silk slippers became my undoing. I slipped in a patch of mud.

He sauntered over, looking down at me like I was a wounded animal.

"Tsk, tsk, tsk. Get up," he commanded. "Get up and run. I like a little exercise before my meal."

I kept my eyes on him as I slowly stood, careful to not lose my footing again. As I put my weight on my feet, I realized what he already knew. I was injured. I hurt my ankle. I *was* a wounded animal.

"Run, sweetheart, run!" he said gleefully.

As my adrenaline kicked in, I was able to ignore the pain. I started to run, but I knew it was a waste. He was toying with me. It didn't matter how far I got or how fast I could go, he could catch me whenever he wanted.

Realizing my fate, I wondered what would happen if I died in that time. Would I awaken in the present like this was a bad dream? Or would dying here in the past kill me? As tears stung my eyes, I knew I was about to find out.

Julien warned me that coming back was dangerous. *Was this how I died to begin with?* I looked towards the castle, which was still glowing with its candlelight and warmth. I was supposed to be in there with Julien. What happened that I was outside?

As tears blurred my vision, the vampire's icy hands wrapped around my neck. He yanked me towards him like a rag doll.

I screamed. I shrieked with every cell in my body. I pushed him away, pressing my hands into his solid body, but he didn't budge. He was cold, he was as hard as marble, and he reeked of rotting flesh. This wasn't how I imagined dying, but there was nothing I could do to save myself.

He jerked me around to face him. His large eyes were jet black. I squeezed my eyes shut, not wanting to stare at the devil, but not knowing what was happening was worse.

The moonlight glinted against the points of his teeth as they came closer to me. He was toying with me, prolonging my death, torturing me. He could have done it quickly, but he was enjoying his game. As his cold breath brushed against my skin, I heard a noise come from the chateau.

"Leave her alone!" Julien commanded.

The vampire scoffed before sinking his teeth in, his eyes on Julien. As Julien ran over, he tackled him, and the vampire loosened his grip on me. I hobbled away from the vampire as quickly as I could.

"Ahh, the master of the castle," the vampire said. "I've been waiting for you. It was your selfishness that brought me here. I knew that if I was patient enough, you would realize that your tasty morsel was missing."

Julien punched the vampire with all his might, but the vampire just laughed at him.

"Let me save you some energy," the vampire said. "There is nothing you can do to hurt me. The longer you make this take, the higher the chances are that after I kill you, I'm going to make your fiancée there my dessert."

"Leave her alone," Julien growled.

"Or what?" The vampire chuckled as he rubbed his chin. As he surveyed Julien, he tilted his head to the side. "I find you humans interesting. My only memories of being human are the warmth of a mother. It's ironic that that woman I call Mother is nothing like that. She's just another witch who thought she could control me. But that's a story for another time."

He looked from Julien, to me, then back at Julien again. Slowly he started to nod as he came to a decision.

"You never answered my question," he said as he tapped the sharp point of his chin. "What are you going to do to stop me?"

Julien rushed at the vampire again, trying to knock him off balance. It was useless. The vampire was too strong.

"Lilac, run!" he commanded. "Get into the house. Tell Alexander, get Hugo! They'll help me. Most importantly, get yourself inside. I need you safe."

"No! I'm not going to leave you here to die," I said.

"It doesn't matter what happens to me," he said. "All that matters is that you're protected. I need to know you're safe." He turned to the vampire, keeping himself between the vampire and myself. "Take me as your victim. Kill me, just leave her alone."

I ran towards the chateau as fast as I could. I didn't want to leave him, but I couldn't let Julien down. I turned back to check on him and watched as Julien lifted a thick branch and swung it at the vampire. He lifted his hand and easily crushed it in the air, shattering it into pieces.

"I was hoping you would do that," he scoffed. "Some of my tastiest treats have been lovers. And I'm sure the two of you would prove to be very delicious indeed. Alright, I won't kill her, but I don't think I'm going to kill you either," he said to Julien. "I think it'll be more fun to give you the immortal kiss. It'll be worse for you if I let you live."

I couldn't move. *Was he going to change Julien? Was this how he became a vampire?*

"Run, Lilac! Please go," Julien begged.

I wanted to run. I heard his words and every part of me wanted to do what he said. But I couldn't. I couldn't leave him with that killer. There was nothing I could do to help him, except for running into the house like he wanted. But I was frozen to the spot.

As the vampire sank his teeth into Julien's neck, he cried out in pain. Julien's sea blue eyes were locked on mine. As the vampire removed his teeth from him, Julien's eyes turned from the sea blue I loved to the icy blue of the vampire I met days before.

"Go!" Julien howled.

He collapsed as he writhed in agony. I wanted to run to him and take away his pain. There had to be something I could do, but I still couldn't move.

The vampire kneeled in front of him and lifted Julien's chin to look at him with his long finger.

"I forgot to mention a little something about the immortal kiss," the vampire said. "Your feelings towards me reflect the vampire you'll become. When I passed the gift to you, all of your hatred for me became an uncontrollable monster inside of you. The only way that you can contain that beast is by having your first meal." His lips tugged up into a sinister smile. "In moments, you will be unable to control yourself. If you haven't pieced it together, your first meal will be your lovely fiancée."

Julien opened his mouth to scream, but instead gasped in pain as death overtook him. He turned to look at me and I knew he wanted me to run. He wanted to tell me to get as far away as I could, but then something changed. His skin blanched and his eyes rolled back.

"Remember I agreed to let her go? I said I wouldn't kill her, and I'm not going to. You saved her from me, dear Julien. It's a shame you can't save her from yourself."

His words were enough to knock the shock out of me. I ran as fast as I could to the entrance of the chateau.

Julien pounced on me like a lion attacking his prey. He flipped me over onto my back so that I was looking up at him. Hovering over me was the man I fell in love with without even knowing him. He was the man I gladly went back in time for after one magical kiss.

I stared up at him, wishing I had listened to him, wishing I had run when I had the chance. I now understood when he warned me of the danger of coming back to the past, that he was trying to protect me from the monster he became.

He bellowed with a mixture of pain, sorrow, and hunger. For a moment I thought I saw sadness flash across his face, but then it turned to stone. He was fighting with himself, wrestling with the hatred that made him. He didn't want to kill me, but he didn't have a choice.

Something flashed through the woods. As Julien struggled with his desire to drain me, he was lifted into the air and thrown towards the older vampire, who was quietly making his escape.

I couldn't focus on anything, it was happening so fast. Everything was just a blur.

Suddenly I was being lifted into Julien's arms, the Julien that I knew in my present. We ran into the chateau and without a word, he carried me upstairs towards the ballroom. As he strode down the hall, the chateau wobbled, then became worn. We were back in the present.

I threw my arms around him. I didn't know how I would ever be able to repay him. I was grateful that he showed up and rescued me. I was grateful that he knew me well enough to know I would go back in time after he told me not to.

"You saved me," I said. "Thank you. I don't know what I would have done if you didn't come."

"You should have never been there," he snarled as he lowered me onto the floor in front of my room.

He vanished before I could say anything else.

CHAPTER 9

I stood up and started walking towards the main hall. I didn't need to see him leave, I know which direction he went. I wasn't going to let him shut me out. I needed answers. Now.

As I entered the main hall, I spotted him entering the other wing. His body was tense with anger. I could've caught up with him, but I was too frustrated from everything I had already been through the night.

"You can't just walk away like that," I said. "Things happened tonight that I need answers to. You have to tell me. How can you expect me to stay here if you're going to be like this? How can I trust you if all you do is run away?"

He spun around on his heel and glared at me.

"How dare you question me!" he roared. "Who told you to not to go back? Who told you it was dangerous?" He paused as stepped closer to where I was standing. "All I've ever done is try to protect you, try to keep you safe, and what did you do? You went behind my back. You went against what I said. You died that night!"

"No, I didn't," I said. "You saved me." Slowly the realization of what happened in the past sank in. That night wasn't just the night he became a vampire, it was the night he lost his love. I felt awful for making him relive that. "I'm sorry, Julien. How could I know? There's just so many things going on right now. Between my mother and now being here with you, there's been so many crazy and unexplainable things. I don't understand it. I don't see how all of it could be real. You have to realize that no normal person would ever understand what happened. But I'm trying to." Our eyes met as he came closer. "I just need a little bit more."

He lowered his head so our foreheads touched, then wrapped his arms around me as he pulled me in close.

In a blink, we were on the ballroom balcony overlooking the wooden area. He didn't say anything, but his eyes revealed his sorrow. He pointed to a small clearing to the side of the balcony leading to the castle's entrance.

"It happened right there, just not here, it was in France. After what happened, I commissioned the oil painting, then locked my memories of that night away. Even though it was real to you, it wasn't. You weren't really in the past.

"That night haunted me. I couldn't stop myself from seeing it, so I locked it away. I locked up my memories in the room."

"But how?" I asked.

"I don't know," he said as he looked down. "I don't really understand how it happened, but that old gypsy woman came back the next day."

Julien shook his head, then met my gaze. His eyes were filled with sadness.

"I will tell you everything you want to know. I will answer all of your questions, but only this one time." He cupped my face in his hands. "I can't keep reliving it."

I had so many questions, and I didn't know where to begin. In my mind, I made a list of them and chose the one that kept popping up the most.

I was afraid to ask him, but I knew if I didn't ask him now, I would never get the chance again. This was my chance to find out, and I wanted to know. I needed to know. I needed to know more about him. I needed to understand everything.

"Did you kill me?" I whispered.

He closed his eyes and took a long breath before opening them again.

"Yes, but I didn't have a choice. I didn't have control of myself. I'm sorry. I told you to run. It wasn't much, but it was the best I could do. I will never forget that night."

I looked up into his icy blue eyes and his cold hard face. Despite his being a vampire, I swore I could still see the human in him. I didn't want to hurt him or make him relive memories he spent so much time trying to forget. But I needed to know more. I needed the whole story.

"Tell me about that night," I said. "I need to know what happened. I need to know all of it."

CHAPTER 10

Julien

The last thing I wanted was to relive that night, especially when I just experienced it only minutes before.

I couldn't blame her. In the past few days, she lost what was left of her family and would have to start her life over again. How could I expect her to live with a vampire in a house that had been keeping its inhabitants alive for over 200 years? I should have known better than that.

She deserved to know the truth. She needed to know everything.

19th Century France

The engagement party was in full swing at Chateau du Soleil. The only thing missing was my fiancée. I checked in with Alexander, who was greeting the guests at the front door.

"Has she arrived yet?" I asked.

"No, sir," he said. "Not yet."

Another hour had passed before I saw her. Her black hair was swept up into place with a diamond and pearl comb I gave her on our first date.

I followed her through the crowd, mesmerized by her beauty like I always was. But it wasn't just that my Lilac was gorgeous, she was smarter than me. Most men wouldn't put up with a woman who had her own thoughts and opinions, but I wanted more than just a pretty face.

When I caught up to her, all I could think about was holding her. I had the violins start so we could dance and I could steal her embrace, but it wasn't enough.

I wanted to be alone with her. I considered ending the party and sending everyone home, but I didn't want to deal with the scandal that would cause. Instead, I suggested we get some fresh air on the balcony.

I didn't see the old woman until after she tugged on my sleeve. It wasn't uncommon for women to want a dance with me, but at my own engagement party, when my betrothed had just arrived, I couldn't oblige her.

The woman's empty threat surprised me, but I could tell Lilac was upset. We continued onto the balcony, but my beloved had such a tender heart that she insisted I dance with the old witch right away.

As Lilac disappeared into the crowd to find her, I stayed behind. I watched her weave through the guests as she hunted for the old gypsy, but eventually I lost sight of her. Every person I passed, I asked if they had seen her, but no one had seen Lilac since we danced.

The longer she was missing, the more frantic I became. I couldn't explain why I was so worried about her being gone, but I needed to find her immediately.

I rushed down the staircase to ask Alexander if he had seen her, but he was nowhere to be found. He never left his post. Something was wrong.

My instincts told me to head outside. I stepped out the door and spotted the old woman before she disappeared into the woods. Something called to me like a siren's song. I followed it towards the clearing by the side of the chateau and found Lilac in his evil embrace.

I offered myself to the vampire to save Lilac, but by the time I realized it was a trap, it was too late. My darling was frozen, rooted to the spot, unable to run. I couldn't do anything more to save her and by the time she regained the ability to escape, she had to defend herself against me.

I was conceived with hatred. I despised him for wanting to feast off Lilac. I resented him for ruining all of our plans and everything I had looked forward to. But I hated myself more for not being able to fight the monster I became: the beast who enjoyed the taste of her sweet blood.

***

After grieving for weeks, I went in search of my maker. I intended on killing him or myself in the process. I was powerful. I knew he was strong too, but I wanted to destroy him for what he did. If it meant I died, then that was even better.

I didn't believe in my own immortality. I didn't want it.

What was the point in living forever if I couldn't be with the woman I loved?

After I quenched the monster's thirst, I looked for the vampire who gave me the immortal kiss, but he was gone. There was no trace of him, no sign of him anywhere. But I had to admit I didn't look too hard. I had to get back to her.

Devastated, I carried Lilac's remains into the house. Hugo helped me care for what was left. It was the worst thing I ever had to do. I spent centuries trying to get past the pain that was in my heart. Only I didn't have one anymore and with Lilac gone, I didn't need it.

I fired every person who worked at Chateau du Soleil. I didn't want anyone around. I didn't want anyone to see what kind of monster I had become.

Hugo and Alexander refused to leave. And despite how often I told Elyse that I didn't need a cook anymore, she refused to leave too.

After telling them everything, Hugo took it upon himself to find the old woman. Using what the vampire said about her, he found her easily. While there were plenty of witches in France in the 1800s, not many of them were bound to a vampire like she was.

The old witch's name was Henriette, and she lived on the outskirts of town in a small cottage. She had a reputation for making curses and creating potions for money.

Five years before, the man she loved had been killed by a vampire. Using her abilities, she aged herself, hopeful she would die soon, then tracked down the vampire and placed a curse on him. Unfortunately things didn't work out exactly as she planned. Consumed by sorrow, Henriette accidentally bound the vampire to her.

While the vampire called her Mother to mock her appearance, he would do almost anything for her. She found victims for him in the hopes that he would honor her wish and kill her.

Although Henriette didn't have any issue with getting him victims, choosing lovers was always hard on her. Every time she found a new couple for him to feed on, she remembered losing her love. It made her hate the vampire even more than she ever had, but they were bound together by their curse and neither could get away.

Hugo took me to visit Henriette as soon as the sun set. I didn't fully know my strengths or my weaknesses by then, but I knew enough about vampires that I didn't want to test if I was immune to the sun or not.

Henriette was expecting us. When we arrived, she was outside of her humble home collecting her laundry. Despite her frail appearance, she carried several baskets on her back into her small cottage before coming back out again. She folded her arms across her chest while chewing on the inside of her cheek as she narrowed her eyes at me.

"So, he didn't kill you," she said.

"No, he didn't," I said. "I wish he had. Instead he gave me what he called the immortal kiss."

Henriette snickered as she clasped her hands together, looking delighted

"I have to admit I'm surprised," she said. "I didn't think he could do that to me anymore. He must be getting soft."

"Soft? He gave me the immortal kiss so I would kill Lilac. He promised he would let her run." Talking about that night was like ripping the scab off a wound. "I made a deal with him. I told him to take me and let her live."

"You bargained with the devil." She shrugged. "There's only one definite that comes when you bargain with the devil. You lose."

"How would you know?" I asked.

"Why do you think I'm standing here talking to you now?"

She waved us into the cottage, where she stirred the contents of a bubbling pot. The scent of sandalwood filled the air.

"What kind of magic is that?" Hugo asked.

"This is not magic at all, just fragrance." She cackled before pulling out a heavy wooden rocking chair and sitting down. "I made a bargain with him years ago and we ended up bound together for life. You never want to be bound for life to someone who cannot die."

"So why don't you change that?" I asked.

"Don't you think I would if I could? You might be my only chance. I don't think he's ever made another vampire before. Right now he's weak. Creating a vampire, especially one out of hatred, is tiresome. The biggest mistake he's ever made was not feeding before creating you." She pointed a crooked finger in my direction. "He used all of his energy to vanish, but he didn't have enough strength to feed after that."

"And how do you know this, old woman? How do I know you're not just saying this? What if you're setting me up?"

"You don't have to know anything. You don't have to trust me, you don't have to believe me," she said. "But I have something you want."

I gritted my teeth as I growled at her. I could feel my hunger deepening inside of me and I knew I would have to eat soon.

She raised an eyebrow, looked at me, and nodded her head.

"You still need to feed. You're young, you need to feed every night. You might not want to, but you don't have a choice if you want to survive."

"I don't need to feed. What I need is to find out how I can kill that vampire who created me."

Henriette sighed as she leered at me. "You are quite the handsome devil, you know that? It's a shame you didn't give me that dance I wanted."

"Stop playing your games with me, hag."

She grimaced before narrowing her eyes at me.

"You might want to think about why you're here before you start calling me names," she said. "Part of being a vampire is that you are immortal, but I can change that. I can make it so that you will die just like everyone else."

"What are you talking about? How can I be immortal yet die?"

Henriette chuckled wildly as she leaned back and rocked. The creaking of her rocking chair shot through my head painfully. She could tell it was bothering me, and it only made her rock even faster.

"Your hearing is becoming more sensitive," she explained. "So tell me, are you willing to trust me?"

She was promising the one thing that would bring me close to Lilac again, my death.

"What do you want?" I asked.

"What I want is exactly what you came here for. I want him dead. I want you to destroy him. And I know how you can do that."

"What's the catch? Remember, you told me to never bargain with the devil, and yet you're bargaining with me."

"But you aren't the devil, my dear," she said with a grin.

"I'm not, but I believe you are."

The corners of her lips turned up sheepishly. I struck a chord with her. I said something she couldn't deny.

"You are much more astute than I thought," she said. "But we're not here to discuss my past, we're here to correct my error. The offer remains-- kill him and you will lose your immortality."

"And what else?"

"There's nothing more," she said. "You have my word."

I eyed her as I tried to figure out exactly what she wanted. I had no doubt in my mind that I would be able to kill my maker. What I doubted was whether making a bargain with her was foolish or not.

"I want something else." I said.

"You're a greedy one. What is it you want besides dying?"

"I want to forget. I want to forget that night. I want to forget everything that happened after I danced with Lilac."

She shook her head sadly. "I wish I could help you with that. If I could help you with that, I wouldn't be where I am today." She let out a long breath. "I would give up my soul for all eternity if only I could forget." She slowly rocked her chair as sadness covered her face.

I sensed her emotions and felt her thoughts. *Another vampire curse,* I thought. She didn't want to be there anymore. She didn't want to think about her own past or the life she left long ago.

"I can't make you forget what happened, and trust me, you don't want to. But I can give you a chance at happiness again," she said. "I can lock your memories of that night away. I can seal them up so that no one will ever be able to access them, not even you." She nodded, pleased with her idea. "But I need to tell you one more thing. Your Lilac will one day come back."

"What do you mean she's going to come back?" I asked.

"You both made a promise to each other. You might not have been able to fulfill that promise by getting married, but the promise was made in your heart. Tell me, the other night when you feasted on your woman, when you mutilated her body with your monstrous teeth, did you destroy your heart?"

I turned away. I didn't want to think about that or I would relive it every time I closed my eyes. Of everything that happened that night, seeing her remains was what haunted me the most. I could handle a taste for blood, or the feel of that warm liquid passing down my throat, giving me new life. What I couldn't accept was the beast that I became.

I rose from my chair and walked out of her cottage into the night air. The cool air felt good as it tousled my hair around. *Give me strength.* I took a deep breath, something that was now simply being a human, and re-entered the cottage again.

"Her heart is intact." I said.

She clapped her hands together and smiled happily.

"Then you leave it up to me," she said. "You will forget those horrific memories from last night until you need to."

My mind swam with questions. I knew there was a catch. I knew there had to be something that she wasn't telling me, but I couldn't piece it all together.

"You said if I kill your vampire, I will lose my immortality. If that's the case, then why would I wait for my Lilac? Wouldn't that mean that I should let your vampire live?"

"You still don't trust me. That's fine, it's perfectly understandable. And if I was in a worse mood, you probably shouldn't trust me. But I like you. And giving you what you want gives me what I want. You'll be giving me my freedom. That's something I haven't had for a very long time."

She rose from her rocking chair and lit a couple of extra candles to give more light to the room. The shadows danced along the wall and made her look even older than she already was.

"Some might call this a curse, but I call it a gift. I'll tell you where the vampire is. I will tell you where to find him and you can figure out the rest.

When the time is right, your Lilac will be reborn wherever you have your castle."

"Wherever? Are you suggesting that I move the castle?"

She nodded. "That vampire has been tormenting the countryside for centuries. When you kill him, everyone will know. Every life that he has touched will be released from his clutches. And with you having to feed and learning how to control your new senses, it is best if you found a place to live where you can find peace."

"Thank you," I said, humbled by her reaction.

"Don't thank me yet," she said. "Since you asked what the catch is, and since you've been so nice, I'm going to tell you what that is now." She paused as she looked outside, then back at me again. "Even after his death, you will be immortal. But once she has returned to the chateau, you will only have 10 days for her to accept your immortal kiss."

"Or what happens?" I asked, feeling satisfied I was right.

"If she accepts it with love, then she will be powerful without the pain and sorrow you experienced. If she accepts it with love, you will share your immortality together."

"What else do I need to know?" I asked.

"The final thing you need to know about is the key. For every curse, for every wish, for each spell or potion, there is always an antidote. The antidote in this curse is a thick glass skeleton key." She waved her hand in the air and a ghostly image of a grinning key appeared. "I have no control over it; no one knows who does. But it makes itself seen by those who need it most. I have a feeling it will unlock the memories you've asked to forget."

Present Day

I leaned against the balcony and pulled Lilac against me, feeling her heart call the vampire inside me. I told her a lot of things that were difficult to understand. There were plenty of times that I couldn't understand it myself. But there was one thing that Lilac could answer.

"Where's the key?" I asked.

She looked up at me, her eyelashes fringed with tears. I could see her searching her memory for it but not finding it.

"I don't know. I left it in the door. I was so excited to go back and see you, to be held by you, to dance with you, that I didn't think to take it with me."

I nodded my head slowly. I knew the key was gone before she even said anything.

"What happened to the witch? Did you ever see her again?" Lilac asked.

"No," I said. "After I killed the vampire who made me I went back to her cottage, but she wasn't there. The cottage looked like it hadn't been used in ages. I had no idea how to find her again, and I didn't care. I was ready to forget."

While I told her the whole story, I left out a couple of things, including the fact that I was dying. My days were numbered, but I couldn't risk her saying that she would take my immortal kiss without her really being in love. It was something that she needed to do on her own. I wasn't as selfish as I once was, nor as conceited to believe that she would fall in love with me so quickly.

If I died without giving her the immortal kiss, I would still die a happy man. Just having these days with her again was enough to bring me joy.

CHAPTER 11

Julien

The next day I was in the library when Hugo knocked on the door. I turned, feeling confused. It wasn't like him to knock before entering. We had all grown so familiar with each other in the centuries since they stayed that their formalities had gone a long ago. Hugo knocking on the library door told me that something was on his mind.

"It's not like you to keep your thoughts to yourself, Hugo," I said.

"Why didn't you tell her everything? I found her for you, sir. I sought her out on the worst day imaginable, her mother's funeral."

"I never told you to find her. I knew she was alive. I had wanted to see her for so many years, but I couldn't."

"Are you afraid of death? Please remember it's not just you here."

I wasn't afraid of death. After the night I was changed, I wasn't afraid of anything. Guilt filled me as I thought about everything that happened. I never intended to tie anyone else to this horror with me. And after waiting for so long for Lilac to return, I realized she was better off having her own life than getting mixed up in my hell.

"I'm sorry, Hugo. I have apologized for this countless times. I thought when the witch was placing her spell that it was only on me. I didn't know it was on Chateau du Soleil. Had I known, I would have never agreed to it. It's no different than my not seeking out Lilac. This is my torture, not yours."

"Forgive me, sir. I don't think any of us have ever regretted living for as long as we have, but we never thought we'd be trapped here. I am the only one brave enough to leave, but whenever I do, I age rapidly. We've been loyal and trustworthy servants to you. That alone is why you need to do your part in helping us."

"I'm not going to tell her," I growled.

"You must!" he exclaimed as his face reddened with exasperation. "You have to tell Lilac that she can save you, that she can save us all. She needs to know. Do you think she hasn't seen you deteriorating in the days since she arrived? Imagine if she knew she could stop that. She should be able to make a fully informed decision, sir."

I turned my back to him and paced the floor.

"You don't understand, Hugo. You don't know what it's like. You and the others had gained immortality just by living in Chateau du Soleil. You are free to come and go as you please, albeit with consequences. But remember, none of you have to deal with my thirst. I'd rather die than let anyone agree to this hell."

"But Julien, while Alexander, Elyse, and I are tied to the chateau, it is tied to you. If you die, we all die."

"Then we'll finally be released from this nightmare," I said.

Hugo slammed his fist against the desktop. Anger consumed him. I felt sorry for putting him through so much rage, but he and I would have to agree to disagree. He thought I was being selfish and thinking about myself when I was really thinking about her. I was thinking about finally saving her life. From the first day I met Lilac, I said she was mine. I obsessed about her when we were alive, but since her death she occupied my thoughts even more.

"Then why bring her here?" he asked.

"I didn't bring her here, remember? That was something you and Alexander planned together with Elyse's help."

"But you wanted to see her again. You've been waiting for her for all this time."

"Yes, I've dreamed about the day I would see her again, but I was satisfied with being able to close my eyes and be with her. Since the moment I discovered she was alive, I wanted to see her, I wanted to touch her delicate skin and bathe in her sweet scent. But all of that is because I love her." I turned to look at Hugo again to make sure he understood. "It is because I love her that I don't want her to be a part of this. It is because I love her that I chose to let her live her life. Now if you will excuse me, there is something that I have to do."

I walked out of the library and headed straight for the dining room where I knew Lilac was busy sketching her plans for the chateau. I didn't have the heart to tell her she was wasting her time. There was only one thing she could do to save my home, and it was the same thing that would save my life. But I refused to tell her what that was.

As I entered the room, she looked up and happiness spread across her face. I couldn't tell her why they brought her here. I wouldn't tell her the future was dependent on her. My dying was a secret I couldn't share with her. All I wanted was to see her smile. I would accept any pain, any death, as long as she was happy.

"You've been working too much," I said.

I pulled out the chair next to her and sat facing her. I closed my hands around hers and soaked in the warmth of her hands against the cold of my hard skin. She threw her head back and laughed.

"What do you mean I'm working too much? I haven't even been here a week."

"It's just with everything that you've gone through and everything that you've had to deal with in the past week, I think you need a little time away. You mentioned your friend Robin in Arizona. I'm sure she would love it if you visited her for a little while."

Her brow wrinkled confusion. She studied my eyes like she used to do in the past, and I wondered how much of her prior life she remembered.

"Are you trying to get rid of me?" she asked.

"No, my love. The last thing I want is to lose you."

My words were saying more than what she asked, but I wanted to make sure that she understood how I felt about her.

"Then why are you sending me away?" she asked.

"I'm not. You are free to come and go as you please. I just thought you would like to visit your friend. Take a break, a little vacation, whatever you want to call it."

She shook her head and I realized I needed to push her to go. I couldn't let her see me get worse. I didn't want her to see me die.

"Think about it," I said. "Next time you talk to Robin, you can bring it up. I'm sure she'll convince you to go."

"I'm sure she will try," she said. "The problem is I'm not sure I want to go."

I didn't wait for her to say anything more. I left the dining room to create distance between us. Any longer in her presence and I would convince her to stay with me and never leave. Now that I had Lilac back, I didn't want to let her go. I didn't want to die anymore. I wanted her to accept my immortal kiss and stay with me. I wanted to hold her. I wanted to love her. Always. But I couldn't do that to her. It wasn't meant to be.

CHAPTER 12

"I can't believe I had to convince you to visit me," Robin said as we walked out of the airport and towards the parking garage. "I haven't seen you in years. You haven't had any time to yourself, or any kind of break probably since before college. And yet I still had to beg you to come out here. What gives?"

Robin's curly red hair was parted in the middle and braided. She had on a pair of shorts and a tank top she had squeezed her breasts into. That was the problem with living in the desert, there were times of the year when you had to wear as little as possible. In comparison, I looked like I was ready for a blizzard with my cropped jeans, black t-shirt, and cardigan. It didn't matter how hot it was, I always ended up cold.

Hearing Robin rant was not the way I wanted to start my time away. I loved her, she and I had always been close, but if she was going to start by making me feel bad, I might as well turn around and fly stand-by back to Virginia.

"I don't know, I just didn't feel like traveling," I said. "Flying out here takes all day."

"Nah, you're not telling me something," she said.

I looked at her as we got into her car, and she smiled. Robin always knew when I was keeping something from her. We could both read each other like an open book.

"I wish I could tell you, but it's confusing even to me," I said. "I know you think I'm crazy, but there is something about Julien. I can't explain it, but I didn't want to leave."

I hated leaving Julien and the castle. No matter how many times he pushed me to go, regardless of how much begging Robin had done, something inside me said *don't go*. I was usually a logical person so since I couldn't figure out what was making me feel that way, I went on the trip. There was no logical reason to not go. It was time for me to stop listening to my emotions and get back to what made sense.

"I can't believe everything that's happened in this short amount of time," I said.

"If you and I weren't so close, I don't think I could tell you this," she said. "But I think you're making a mistake. It's just not like you to fall for a guy like this. And I can't help but think you're on some kind of rebound or something."

I didn't answer her. I didn't know what to say. Thinking about everything that had gone on in the past week, I knew that anyone would think I was crazy. Sometimes *I* thought I was crazy. But Robin didn't know the whole story. If she knew everything, she would understand. She was my closest friend and I needed someone to talk to. I was almost desperate for it.

Robin shook her head sympathetically at me as she started the car. I knew there was a lot more that she wanted to say, but it would have to wait. She knew me well enough to know that pushing me wasn't the way to get me to talk.

As we left the airport, we headed south to Robin's apartment in Tempe, I looked at the cactus and rocky mountains surrounding us. I loved Arizona, I loved being out west. But it never fully felt like home, not like Virginia.

I tried to focus on the beautiful surroundings, but I couldn't get Julien out of my mind. He seemed so sad before I left. If he weren't a vampire, I would have asked him if he wasn't feeling well. His skin was losing the white luster it had the first night we met, and he looked tired and weak. I didn't know if he had been feeding or not, he never mentioned it to me when he went out. But the longer I was at the chateau, the worse he seemed to appear.

I'd be lying if I didn't admit that was one of the reasons I flew to Arizona. I thought Julien might be better off without me.

"Hey, I bet you're hungry," Robin said. "And I know you must be missing Burger Bash. How about we stop off and get some burgers, fries, and shakes just like old times?"

"Yeah, that sounds great," I said. "I could really go for that right now."

She turned off the freeway and drove to the nearest Burger Bash, the same one we used to go to all the time in college. The place hadn't changed a bit. The restaurant was still starkly white with splashes of red tile. The thumping of the fry chopper continued in the background. Even though it was barely noon, the place was already packed.

As we sat down with our food, I felt the weight of all the changes that I had gone through in the past week finally hit me. I had to talk to someone. I needed to tell Robin not only about all the crazy stuff that happened, but also how happy I was.

I took a long sip of my chocolate shake as I tried to build up the courage to tell her what was really going on with me. Across the table, I could tell she was waiting to hear my story. She knew I wanted to talk, I just hoped she wouldn't freak out when I told her the truth.

"There's so much I have to tell you, Robin," I said. "But you're never going to believe any it."

"Try me," she said. "You know all about my crazy family, I don't think you could tell me something that I haven't heard before."

I laughed. "You're right, your family has had some really crazy stories, but nothing like this."

She munched on her French fries as I tried to figure out the best way to tell her about Julien. But every way I imagined telling her the story made it sound crazier and crazier.

Now that I was so far from him, I began wondering if I had made everything up. Maybe everything really was just a dream. Maybe I was suffering the way my mother suffered and now I didn't know what was real and what was fantasy. That made it even more important to talk to someone who knew the difference. When it came down to it, just getting to the point was probably the best way to tell her.

"Do you believe in vampires?" I asked.

"Vampires? You mean pale skin, undead, sharp teeth, has an appetite for blood vampires?"

Just hearing her break it down like that made me realize how much crazier it sounded. Still, I needed to talk to someone. I needed a friend.

"Yes, that's exactly it. Vampires. Like Dracula, but not like Edward Cullen. There's no sparkling going on."

She laughed. "What do vampires have to do with anything?"

"Julien is a vampire."

Robin stared at me for a minute. She didn't move, she didn't even twitch. My words had turned her into stone. Slowly, the shock left her face and she blinked at me before taking a long drink from her strawberry shake.

"You've got to be shitting me," she said. "You know he's lying to you, right? Seriously, that's the craziest thing I've ever heard. He must be married."

"Married? Where do you even get that from?" I asked.

Robin confused me. Believing someone was a vampire was hard, I knew that, but I couldn't follow how she thought Julien was married when I was living in his home.

"Because I've heard of guys making up some tall tales to get what they want from women. I've never heard anyone claim to be a vampire, but why else would someone say that?"

"Maybe because it's true?"

"How do you know? Did you see him kill someone?"

The memory of him attacking me after he changed flashed in my mind. It wasn't his fault, he couldn't control himself, but I knew what happened to me that night two hundred years before. But how could I explain that?

"Not exactly," I said

"What do you mean not exactly? You either did or you didn't. Did you see him kill someone?"

"I can't really explain." I shook my head as I thought about all the options I had of telling her about my past at the chateau. I didn't know what she would believe and despite my wanting to follow logic, my instinct was telling me to shut up.

I didn't want to tell her any more about Julien and I. I didn't want whatever negative thing she might say tainting how I felt about Julien.

"I know he's a vampire. I know vampires drink blood to survive."

She leaned across the table and grabbed my hand

"Listen, Lilac, you know I love you, but this is some crazy shit you're talking," she said. "There's no freaking way that this man is a vampire. They do not exist." She punctuated her sentence by squeezing my hand. "I don't know why you think he drinks blood, maybe he said he's a vampire, I don't know. What I do know is that you need to stop and think about what you're doing with him. Because no matter what, that man is telling you that he is a killer."

"No, he's not like that at all. I knew you wouldn't understand."

"I *do* understand. You've been through a lot. You left everything to take care of your mom, and now she's passed away. She died in her sleep and you weren't even in the apartment. You think I don't know the guilt you're feeling because of that? You know you don't have to say anything, but I know that deep down you're blaming yourself for her being gone. You're like a battered woman, Lilac. I just don't think you're thinking straight anymore."

I was done. I hadn't been back in Arizona for an hour and I already regretted being there. I regretted opening my mouth, of telling the only friend that I had left about my life. I looked at the time and wondered when the next flight back would be. I wanted to get back to Julien. I wanted to get back to the chateau. It was my new home.

"I'm sorry, Robin." I said. "I don't think this was a good idea after all. I know you're only saying those things because you care about me, and I know that what I told you is hard to accept, and it's hard to understand. Right now I just need you to be a friend and to listen. I know it all sounds crazy but this is what I was meant to do, this was where I was meant to be. Everything in my life has led up to being at the chateau and being with Julien."

Robin shook her head. "Then we're just going to have to agree to disagree."

"Take me back to the airport, I'm going home."

"Oh come on, Lilac," she said, looking disappointed. "That's fine if you want to go back, but you flew all the way out here. Just spend the day, I know we just had lunch, but stay through dinner. You can take a red eye back." She reached across the table again and squeezed my hand. "Please, Lilac. As your friend, just take this one day and don't think about him. Spend a few hours with me, and then you can go back to your crazy life and I will pretend that you didn't tell me anything."

Robin looked away from me. I could tell she was lying, but I couldn't figure out why. Was she saying we couldn't be friends anymore? Or was she saying something else?

She was my closest friend, so I had to give her the benefit of the doubt. I squeezed her hand back as I slowly agreed.

"I'll stay through dinner, but only if you stop treating me like something's wrong with me. Give me the benefit of the doubt for once."

***

When we got back to the apartment, I excused myself and went to the guest room. I told Robin I was tired, which I was. It was a long flight and with Julien being up during the night, my body clock had started adjusting so we could spend more time together. After the stress of dealing with Robin, on top of the long flight, I just wanted to take a nap.

I had slept maybe an hour before my cell phone started ringing. I picked it up and saw that it was someone from Chateau du Soleil calling. I had no reason to think it, but I knew something bad had happened.

"Hello?" I said.

"You need to come home," Hugo blurted into the phone. "He's in trouble, they've taken him away."

I jolted upright and swung my legs over the side on the bed.

"What do you mean? Who's taken him?" I asked, trying to stay calm.

My heart raced and I felt my body tremble as my mind raced. How could he be in trouble? Who would've taken him? This wouldn't have happened if I stayed.

"The police. They brought a warrant for his arrest. They're saying he's a killer."

This was my fault. I needed to talk, I needed a friend, and I trusted the wrong person. Robin must have called the cops. I knew she was only trying to protect me, but she still didn't understand that I didn't need protection.

I got up from the bed, put my shoes on, and grabbed my bag.

"Get me home, Hugo. Do whatever you have to, but get me home before dawn. I'm going to the airport right now."

"Yes," he said. "I knew that's what you would say. I arranged for a private jet and it's leaving in an hour. You should land at 1am. I'll be there to pick you up."

I hung up with him and left the guest room. Robin was sitting on the couch watching TV. She turned as I entered the room.

"I thought you would nap longer," she said.

"How could you?" I hissed. "I trusted you. I just needed someone to talk to, I didn't need any kind of protection or advice. I know how crazy everything sounds, but all that matters is that I care about him."

"You're not thinking right, Lilac. I did what I had to do. If you were in my situation, you would've done the same thing."

"I don't think so. I think I would have trusted you more than you've trusted me."

"Don't get all high and mighty on me," she said. "What are you thinking? You said it yourself, he's a vampire. Even if they don't exist, that still makes him a murderer."

"You have no idea what you're talking about. You don't know him like I do." I glared at her as I thought about our long friendship. I was willing to give her one more chance to make things right. "Now if you really consider me your friend, you will drive me to the airport. I'm flying back in an hour. I need to get this straightened out."

"You can't go back," she said, her voice rising hysterically. "He's going to kill you."

"Don't you think he would've done that by now if that was what he intended?"

Using my cell phone, I looked up the nearest taxi service. I gave them a call and told him I needed a ride to the airport right away. I couldn't count on Robin to help me anymore.

I headed towards the door, figuring I would wait outside for the cab. I had nothing more to talk to Robin about and I didn't want to be near her anymore.

"You're not thinking right," she mumbled. "Your mom died and now you're replacing her with this Julien guy. I don't understand it. You're usually so smart, but maybe your mom's passing affected you more than you let on. That's the only logical explanation."

Robin grabbed my arm as I reached the door.

"I'm done with logic, Robin," I said as I yanked my arm away from her. "It might not make sense to you, it might sound crazy even to me, but I know how I feel about him. I know who he really is."

"No, Lilac, you don't. If you did, you wouldn't be protecting a killer."

"Just leave me alone. I never expected you to completely understand. I just expected you to be my friend and support me. You have to just let things be. Because there's no way anything you say right now is going to keep me from going back to Virginia. He's in jail and I need to get him out before sunrise."

CHAPTER 13

The taxi arrived just as I walked out of her apartment. I was surprised that Robin didn't come after me, but it just meant I needed to accept our friendship was over.

I didn't know why I expected her to act differently. I just thought she would care more about how I felt and how happy I was instead of focusing on the fact that Julien was a vampire.

As the cab reached the freeway and headed north towards the airport, my phone buzzed from an incoming call. It was Robin. I didn't want to talk to her, I didn't want to fight anymore. I thought about sending the call straight to voicemail, but I wanted to give her another chance.

"Please don't give me another lecture," I said. "Because right now I'm not even sure that you and I were the kind of friends that I thought we were. I thought we had a different kind of friendship, Robin."

"He's a killer, Lilac," she squawked. "I don't know how many different ways I can tell you that. He is a murderer. When I called the police, they told me they had hundreds of open cases for missing persons and unsolved murders. When I told them that he told you he's a vampire, they started to attribute all of those to him. Each one of those people was killed by this man. You have to understand that you're not safe."

I didn't want to hear it. I knew Julien. I knew he wouldn't kill anyone unless they deserved it. We talked about it, he told me he only fed off of the bad people in society--the child abusers, the rapists, the murderers. He was a vampire, I knew that made him a killer, but that didn't make him a bad person.

"I've had enough of this," I said. "I love Julien. That should have been enough for you if you really cared about me. If you really valued me as your friend, as your sister like you called me so many times before, then all that would have mattered was that I was happy and that I love him. You didn't listen to anything I said. You heard the one thing and ran with it. Don't ever call me again."

I hung up before she could say anything else. I never admitted that I loved Julien before, but I did. I knew Robin would complain that it was too fast and that I was using him to fill some void left by my mother. That was the kind of psychobabble I was used to from her, but I knew how I felt for him had nothing to do with that.

All of this had to do with Julien being the love of my life. If Robin wanted logic, that's where it pointed to. His love brought me back 200 years later. I knew this with a certainty because the more time I spent with him, the more I remembered of my prior life with him. There was no way I was going to let him die because of my mistake. That happened once already. I wasn't going to let it happen again.

***

I was alone in a small private jet flying back to Virginia when the flight attendant handed me the telephone. Unsure who it could be, I put the phone to my ear and listened before I said anything.

I was tired of talking anyway. Talking had only gotten me into more trouble.

"Miss Lilac?" Hugo said. "Are you there?"

"Yes, Hugo," I said. "I'm going straight to the police station when I land. This will be cutting it close with the layover. I heard they're trying to pin some unsolved cases on him. Do you know if they have any evidence? Do they have any witnesses?"

"No, I've always made sure that whatever he did, no traces were left behind."

I remembered the first time I met Hugo and he said he would do anything for Julien. Now I understood how far he would take that. I knew him well enough to know that he might have protected Julien, but he might not have been as careful himself. I worried that he could be implicated if he entered the police station with me.

As the plane began its descent, a flight attendant walked past.

"Where are we?" I asked.

"It's a small plane, miss. We need to refuel several time before we get to our final destination."

As she walked away, I moved the phone back against my cheek.

"Hugo? What happens if he's in the sun?" I asked.

"He dies. New vampires will be destroyed instantly, but if he's touched by the sun, he'll go through a burning process until he dies. But there's more than that to be worried about," Hugo said. "He's weak. He's already dying. He begged me not to tell you."

"What do you mean? How can he be dying?"

"I can't say. I would love to tell you, but he made me swear that I wouldn't. I *will* tell you that you can save him. Only you can save him."

"How?"

"He has to tell you. That can only come from him."

The phone went dead. I tried to call back, but no one answered. In a few hours, I would be back in Virginia, but there wasn't much time. The sun would be rising soon.

***

Hugo waited in the car after driving to the police station. They brought me to the officer on duty that arrested Julien at Chateau Du Soleil. He brought me into a small room with a metal table and a couple of folding chairs. I sat down on one and he sat across from me with a stack of files next to him.

"Thank you for coming in, Miss Martin," he said. "My name is Detective Jack Dalton. I'm in charge of the unsolved cases department. Do you see the stack here? This isn't even the beginning of the files that I have."

"But what right do you have to arrest Julien Lambert?" I asked.

He leaned back in his chair as his belly pushed against the buttons on his snug yellow shirt. He rocked the folding chair on the edges of its legs as he nodded slowly.

"You're right," he said. "I have nothing on him. All I have is a phone call from your friend saying that you said he's a murderer." He tapped his pencil on the table before he continued speaking. "So why don't you tell me why you would say that?"

I knew it was my word against Robin's. The detective wasn't there, he didn't know what was going on.

"If he was a murderer, then would I be here right now? I've been living at his house for the past week. I've been through every room in his house. I spent time with him, and I know this man,

Detective. He is not a murderer. Obviously Robin was mistaken."

He sighed with annoyance.

"There's something about him that doesn't add up," he said. "All of these cases have one thing in common. The victims have been drained of their blood. You never hear about it in the news because every single one of these files belongs to some person who no one cares about if they die."

He pointed to a file on top of his stack and lifted it up so I could read the label. "Pimp." He put the file down on the table and picked up another one. "Dealer."

He set that file down and picked up another one, then waved it in his hand.

"This one is my favorite. This is from way back from before I became a police officer. This one had been handed down to me. I've been going after him for years. He's a serial killer. But before we could get to him, someone else did."

He put the file down on the table and then tapped the top of a taller pile of folders.

"Each and every one of these is not only labeled as having been an undesirable, but they all have a similar cause of death. I have a file room filled with them. As much as I would love to accept your friend's report, there are too many inconsistencies with Mr. Lambert to fit with these murders. What I have here couldn't have been done by your boyfriend. They go back for centuries. And unless there's something about him that we don't know about, some kind of mumbo-jumbo that we all know doesn't really exist, I know that your boyfriend couldn't have done these murders."

"Does that mean he's free to go?" I asked.

The detective nodded slowly. "It's protocol, with such a big body count, that if someone says they have information, we have to follow through. There's no evidence though. I have nothing but her word, which doesn't count for anything. I don't have any evidence to link him to any crime, therefore I have nothing to hold him."

He stood and walked over to the door as he opened it I followed him down the hall to a small cell. The sun was just beginning to rise. Small streams of light were coming through the cell's window, cornering Julien, who huddled against the wall, trying to avoid the growing light. His eyes darted over to me, then a calm smile spread across his face.

He didn't look well. I had only been gone a day, but he looked thin and more pale than usual. In the time that I was gone, he was a ghost of himself.

The detective left us in the cell with the door open and I stepped forward into the sunlight, giving Julien some more shade.

"My wish came true," he said as he forced a smile. "I always dreamed of seeing you in sunlight one more time. I always loved how the sun made your skin glow and how it brought out those delicate red tones in your dark hair."

He held his hand out to me and I took it, careful to keep our connection in the shadows.

"I always loved how the sun made you squint. I know you thought your eyes to be ordinary, since they were brown, but they're not. And when you're in the sun, it changes the brown by making them look like the color of honey. I've never told anyone this before, but about fifty years after you were gone, I started convincing myself that I was making all of that up. But seeing you now, I find you even more beautiful than I remembered."

"They're releasing you. You're free to go," I said, fighting back tears as the sun rose higher.

"It's ironic, no? By releasing me in daylight, they've handed me a death sentence." He grinned, but sorrow still filled his eyes. "It's okay, I'm dying anyway."

"How? How can you be dying? That's not possible."

"I just am. But it doesn't matter, I've embraced it. This past week was more than I could have ever hoped for. More than I ever imagined. It made everything worth it. I'm ready to accept my fate."

Julien got to his feet and stepped forward. "Just let me touch you one last time."

As he reached his other hand towards my cheek, smoke rose from his skin where the sun touched it. He didn't move, he didn't retract it in pain. With all my might, I jumped towards him, pushing him back against the cement walls of the cell and back into the shadows.

"You have to tell me," I demanded. "Hugo said that I can save you. You have to tell me how."

Julien shook his head but wouldn't speak.

"Tell me, Julien. I'd do anything for you. I love you. Tell me how I can save you. If I have to lose you now after all this time, I don't think I could go on."

His eyes showed more life as he examined me. He reached up and gently cupped my face with his hands.

"Say it again," he said. "Tell me what you said. Repeat it. I need to know for sure before I tell you."

"I love you. I love you, Julien. I can't explain it. I don't know how it happened. I have feelings for you that are like memories, but I know they're real."

"I love you too. I've only ever loved you. Always. That's why I didn't want to tell you. I didn't want to tell you why Hugo found you. But I will now. Remember the old hag from the night of our party? I wanted to forget. I didn't want to live without you, so she agreed to put a curse on me. That's how you were able to discover my memories. I'm dying. At best I have a few more days, but you can change that if what you said is true. I didn't want to tell you because I didn't want you to suffer the same way I had. The only way for you to save me is for me to give you the immortal kiss."

"There's a reason I'm here, Julien, whether Hugo found me or not. You said it before about the chateau, you said the others were trapped. Well, I'm trapped too. I'm tied to Chateau du Soleil just like you are, but I love it as much as I love you. We're all tied to it. You said that you became a beast when that vampire gave you his immortal kiss, because you were filled with hatred towards. But what would happen if you gave it to me and I felt nothing but love?"

"I don't know for certain. I just know with the gypsy told me. She was a witch, she was a devil, there's no reason to trust her, but so far everything she told me was true. She said you wouldn't go through what I did. She said things would be different."

"I can't let you die here," I said. "I can't let you die after we've waited so long to be together. If it will save you, then do it. If it means I'll be suffering, then at least I'm suffering with you."

Julien's lips pressed against mine, then he slowly opened my mouth as he kissed me hungrily. I felt a sharp sting on my tongue and then my mouth filled with the warm, coppery taste of my own blood.

Julien pulled away, his eyes as black as coal and his face was stone, but I didn't have any fear. I trusted him. I loved him. I was ready to accept his immortal kiss. As his teeth sank into my neck, I melted into his arms.

CHAPTER 14

I felt the blood draining out of me. My life was slipping away, but I stayed calm. Despite the loss, I was also feeling pleasure I had never experienced before, something greater than I could ever imagine.

As Julien released me, he stepped into the sunlight, drunk from my blood. Nothing happened. He didn't burn, he didn't smoke. Instead his skin changed from the sickly pallor he had before to the vibrant healthy skin of the man I met centuries ago.

He held his hand out to me and I stared in wonder at the man I first danced with in the ballroom. I didn't need his help, but I took his hand and felt his power as he lifted me back to my feet.

I felt stronger and more powerful than I had ever imagined. I understood the cockiness he had when I first met him as a vampire. I felt the confidence of that vampire from 200 years ago that mocked me and told me to run. But as my hunger grew, that strength lessened. I sensed humans nearby who would not be safe from me until I fed.

I didn't feel the pain or the beast that Julien experienced. I didn't become the monster that Julien was, I was simply a hungry newborn.

Hugo appeared in the doorway, looking concerned. His eyes widened as he saw Julien standing in the sunlight, and then he looked over at me with a surprised grin.

"Mon Dieu! I knew it," Hugo exclaimed. "I knew she would do it. I knew she loved you."

Julien spun around and approached Hugo.

"We have to go," he said, worry dripping from his voice. "She needs to feed or she will die."

"But what about the sun?" Hugo asked. "How are you in the sun?"

Julien shook his head "I don't know, but the old hag did say love was the most powerful spell of all."

He reached his hand out to me and I clutched at it as I started to feel weak. I stepped into the sunlight and felt its heat, but it didn't burn me. My skin lightened and I discovered I could hear things I wasn't able to hear before. Feeling dizzy, I stepped closer as Julien wrapped his arms around me, giving me support.

"Use me, Miss. You may drink from me," Hugo said.

"No Hugo, I can't," I said. "You can't sacrifice yourself. I will follow the same rules as Julien. I will find someone who is worthy of death." "

"But you must drink now," Julien said. "The blood is fresh in me so I don't look as pale. Your love is protecting me from the sun, but you are going to continue to get more pale. We can't walk out of the police station with you looking like death. And if you don't feed soon, you will die. I've drained you just to the point of death. You're not fully a vampire until after your first drink."

Hugo stepped forward and took my hand. With his eyes meeting mine, he spoke.

"I trust you, Miss Lilac."

Julien looked outside of the cell to make sure that we were alone. With one swift motion, I carefully sank my teeth into Hugo's neck. His blood was sweet and thick, like drinking honey. His heartbeat pulsed within my veins. I wanted to continue drinking from him. I wanted to drain him, but I needed to control myself. I didn't want to kill Hugo, I owed a lot to him. If it hadn't been for him, Julien and I would have never come together again.

I pushed Hugo away as I wiped my mouth with the back of my hand. The weakness was gone. I felt even stronger. I was invincible.

"Are you alright?" I asked.

Hugo nodded as he rubbed his neck. "I'm fine, you can drink more."

"No," Julien said as he stepped between us. "This isn't the place for this, and any more and you'll weaken. She's had enough to get us out of here without suspicion. I'll take her to feed properly later."

As the three of us made our way out of the police station, one of the patrolmen eyed me curiously.

Are you all right, miss?" he asked. "You look pale."

"I'm fine. This is how I always look," I said.

Julien and I sat in the back of the car as Hugo drove back to the chateau. Julien wrapped his arms around me protectively as I rested my head against his chest.

I knew it was impossible, but I swore I heard his heart beating. I looked up at him with confusion in my eyes, and he met my gaze head on.

"I feel more alive than I have in 200 years," he said. "Love destroyed the curse and it did something miraculous. Here, touch my hand."

He held his hand out to me and I touched it. His skin was soft and warm, almost human. I touched my cheek and felt the heat on my cheeks. As I looked at myself in the reflection of the window, I realized I looked like I always had.

"We did it, Lilac," Julien said excitedly. "We'll finally have our forever. We finally have the rest of our lives together."

EPILOGUE

"Hugo! Hugo, come here," Alexander called from the end of the hall. "I need your help with this."

I hurried over and found Alexander struggling with the large oil painting of Miss Lilac that used to cover the ballroom entrance. He was trying to carry it by himself.

"What are you doing?" I asked, amused as the oversized frame swung dangerously in his arms.

"Well, now that the ballroom is being used again, I thought we should find a better place for this."

"It's too big for you to carry by yourself," I said.

"Are you going to help me or not?" he asked.

I grabbed one end of the frame and the two of us carried it into the main hall. We set it against the empty wall at the top of the steps and Alexander stepped back, wiping his dark blue suit of any dust.

"I think this is the perfect place for it," he said. "What do you think?"

"I think you should leave that decision to Miss Lilac. I'm not sure that she wants a huge painting in front of her every time she comes home."

Alexander rubbed his chin as he nodded slowly. "You have a point. I'll have to figure something else out."

"For now, why don't we leave the painting here," I said. "It's too large to be carrying around everywhere."

"Yes, you're right again," he said. "I hate when you're right, and that's happening more and more. Stop it."

He glanced at me slyly and I scoffed, pretending to be offended. It was part of our usual banter.

"You know, they're dancing right now," he said. "I know how much you enjoy watching them dance."

My brow rose as I listened to him. Watching Julien and Lilac dance had become the highlight of my days. I've never seen such love before, and watching them glide across the dance floor reminded me that everything we went through was worth it.

"Are you going out tonight?" I asked before heading to the ballroom.

"I haven't decided yet," he said. "There's so much to explore."

"I thought we were going to the movies," Elyse said as she entered. "You know I can't get enough of them."

Alexander nodded. "How about it, Hugo? Care to join us?"

"Another time," I said. "My new book is beckoning me. I can't believe how many books fit in this little device." I pulled my Kindle out from underneath my arm and held it up to them. "The book is always better than the movie, you know."

I waited until Alexander and Elyse were gone before I headed to the ballroom and slipped inside, hoping Julien and Lilac wouldn't see me. They were waltzing, as they had done countless times before. I had lost track of the days since Lilac had returned into our lives. Time didn't matter anymore to any of us.

Thinking back to when Lilac arrived, I remembered the castle's disrepair. Incredibly, it didn't look like that anymore. By the time we returned from the police station, the chateau had transformed herself back to a thing of beauty. Gone were the cracks, the faded carpeting and broken tile. Everything looked exactly like I remembered in its heyday.

Julien was dressed in a pale yellow suit reminiscent of the one he wore at their engagement party. Lilac stunned in a replica of the dress she wore in the portrait. They were a handsome couple, and their joy was infectious as they danced to a concerto that played from the brand new sound system.

We were all so much happier now that Lilac was in our lives. Ahh, Lilac. Just the thought of her brought a smile to my face. I was more than happy to take all the credit for her return, even if I had some help.

I would do anything for them, and I had. Whatever they wished for, I would make sure they would get it. As I watched them spin across the dance floor, I opened my hand and looked at the long glass skeleton key for the last time.

"Your work here is done," I whispered.

I held my hand up and I watched the happy couple dance as the key vanished.

About The Author

Liliana Rhodes is a New York Times and USA Today Bestselling Author who writes Contemporary and Paranormal Romance. Blessed with an overactive imagination, she is always writing and plotting her next stories. She enjoys movies, reading, photography, listening to music, and spending time with her son. After growing up in the Northeast, Liliana now lives further south with her husband, son, two very spoiled dogs, and a parrot and a fish who are plotting to take over the world.

Connect Online

www.LilianaRhodes.com

www.facebook.com/AuthorLilianaRhodes